Heirs to an Empire

Succession, Secrets and Scandal

Following the death of their father, English aristocrat Cedric Pemberton, it's time for the Pemberton heirs to stake their claim in the family empire.

From fashion and cosmetics to jewelry and fragrance, Aurora Inc. is a multinational company with headquarters all over the world.

As the siblings take the lead in different divisions of the business, they'll face challenges, uncover secrets and learn to start listening to their hearts...

Gabi and Will's Story

Scandal and the Runaway Bride

Charlotte and Jacob's Story

The Heiress's Pregnancy Surprise

Available now!

And return for more Pemberton adventures in Aurora Inc., coming soon!

Dear Reader,

It's not very often I get to do glamorous things, and quite often I feel like a fish out of water when I do. I've been to New York several times now, and I still get a little awestruck. I've been to Broadway. I dined at The Russian Tea Room with friends. And I've danced the night away in the Twilight Room at the Waldorf, thanks to my publisher's dynamite parties. Each time, I take a moment to look around myself and think, *What am I doing here?*

It is always a pleasure to bring some of those amazing moments to my stories. Jacob Wolfe, bodyguard to VIPs, is hired to keep an eye on Charlotte Pemberton in New York for Fashion Week. While his company guards celebrities and dignitaries the world over, he still feels his place is in the background. That is, until he's at Charlotte's side.

I wrote *The Heiress's Pregnancy Surprise* while I was off work due to COVID-19 closures. The world seemed very different in those weeks and months. I hope this book offers you that bit of respite at the end of a hard day or during rough times.

Best wishes,

Donna

The Heiress's Pregnancy Surprise

Donna Alward

—

Recycling programs for this product may not exist in your area.

ISBN-13: 978-1-335-56686-7

The Heiress's Pregnancy Surprise

Copyright © 2021 by Donna Alward

This edition published by arrangement with Harlequin Books S.A.

For questions and comments about the quality of this book, please contact us at CustomerService@Harlequin.com.

Harlequin Enterprises ULC
22 Adelaide St. West, 40th Floor
Toronto, Ontario M5H 4E3, Canada
www.Harlequin.com

Printed in U.S.A.

Donna Alward lives on Canada's east coast with her family, which includes her husband, a couple of kids, a senior dog and two crazy cats. Her heartwarming stories of love, hope and homecoming have been translated into several languages, hit bestseller lists and won awards, but her favorite thing is hearing from readers! When she's not writing, she enjoys reading (of course), knitting, gardening, cooking...and she is a *Masterpiece Theater* addict. You can visit her on the web at donnaalward.com and join her mailing list at donnaalward.com/newsletter.

Books by Donna Alward

Harlequin Romance

Heirs to an Empire

Scandal and the Runaway Bride

South Shore Billionaires

Christmas Baby for the Billionaire
Beauty and the Brooding Billionaire
The Billionaire's Island Bride

Destination Brides

Summer Escape with the Tycoon

Marrying a Millionaire

Best Man for the Wedding Planner
Secret Millionaire for the Surrogate

Visit the Author Profile page
at Harlequin.com for more titles.

CHAPTER ONE

JACOB WOLFE WAS used to flying first class. What he wasn't used to was sitting next to Charlotte Pemberton.

They were on a late-night flight from London to New York, and all around them people were sleeping, or at the very least had their eyes closed and earbuds in their ears. The cabin lighting was dimmed, and in first class, passengers wore eye masks and were covered with blankets to get some rest.

Not Charlotte. She had her laptop open, a glass of wine beside her and glasses perched on her nose as she worked away on...something. Jacob didn't know what, and didn't much care. His job was to keep her safe, not worry about whatever nonsense she was working on.

It was no surprise that the fashion world was far departed from his normal life. As a former SAS operative, the last thing on his mind was fashion shows and parties and...whatever else the Pembertons got up to in their fancy, extravagant life.

He was a plain guy with simple pleasures, despite running a top security business for VIPs and dignitaries. Over the next nine days, he expected he'd do a lot of internal eye rolling, but Aurora Inc. was a new and big client, and he was being paid extremely well to spend the week babysitting the Earl of Chatsworth's sister. And he'd try not to be too resentful of the fact he'd had to cancel his first vacation in three years in order to make it happen. Just his luck that the man originally assigned to the job had picked up some sort of parasite on his last assignment. He'd be fine, but the treatment meant his staying in the Big Smoke while Jacob flew to the Big Apple.

He was no stranger to sacrifice, and Wolfe Security was his company, so here he was. On a plane to New York. In first class.

It still chafed, though. He'd started the company to protect people from real harm. Not babysit spoiled princesses.

Charlotte picked up her wine, took a sip and then looked over at him. "You're not sleeping?" she whispered.

"Clearly not, miss," he replied.

She frowned, her brows puckering above her

clear frames. "If you call me miss again, we're going to have a problem."

"Noted, ma'am."

She huffed. "Mr. Wolfe. Please just call me Charlotte."

He said nothing and lifted an eyebrow.

She huffed again and turned back to her laptop. "You should order a beer and relax."

"No drinking on the job, miss."

This time she sat back and rested her head against the plush headrest, and then turned so she was looking at him. "This is going to be a very long week if we're always so formal. Look, I don't like this any more than you do. I don't need personal protection. It's ridiculous. But that was a condition of the trip, so here we are."

He met her gaze. "It's not my job to like or dislike anything. It's just my job to do my job."

Which was true, but didn't take into account that Charlotte Pemberton was the most beautiful client he'd ever had. Her eyes were heavily lashed and a unique shade of hazel, leaning toward green but with a gold rim around the iris. Her hair was a smooth and lovely brown and fell just to her jaw, and right now she had the right side tucked behind her ear. Fine cheekbones and the hint of a dimple on one side of her luscious mouth made her seem both refined and with a sense of humor. He surely hoped so. It would be a very long assignment otherwise.

She sighed. "I know. I'm sorry. I'm annoyed with my family for making me do this. I'm not annoyed with you personally."

"Good to know." He couldn't help but smile the tiniest bit. She smiled back, and the awkwardness of the past four hours—from pickup to airport security to the flight—eased just a little bit.

"They've taken a few emails and letters too seriously."

"Better to be safe than sorry." He knew this to be true. He made his living at it.

"I'm not a child. I'm twenty-eight. I don't need to have my life dictated."

"Yes, ma'am."

"Stop ma'aming me."

He grinned. A flight attendant made her way silently through first class and he requested a glass of water. Charlotte waved off a second glass of wine.

Jacob drank his water; Charlotte finished her wine and went back to clicking the keys on her laptop. She wasn't going to sleep, but he was. A few hours of shuteye on the plane meant he'd be alert when they landed. He put his head against the headrest and closed his eyes. Maybe New York wasn't Tenerife, but it could be worse, he supposed. He'd been in some horrible hellholes in his day.

No, New York wasn't a hardship at all. So why was he feeling so off balance?

Charlotte waited until Jacob Wolfe closed his eyes, then finally let out the sigh she'd been holding for hours. When her mother had announced that she was hiring a bodyguard for Charlotte for the Fashion Week trip, she'd rebelled. Hard. She was finally getting a chance to take the lead on something this big and her mother was making her have a babysitter. It was ridiculous.

Even more ridiculous was how freaking gorgeous Jacob Wolfe was. Gorgeous, not pretty, like so many of the men in her line of work. Not that pretty wasn't great; it was. She'd enjoyed being on the arm of pretty men in the past, men with perfect hair and skin and who could step into a designer suit and look like a million dollars. Men who required no emotional attachment. She'd been burned by that before, though, and wasn't in the market to take the leap again.

But Jacob Wolfe was not that kind of man. His suit was perfectly tailored, his tie precisely knotted, even during the long late-night flight. Still, she appreciated his other attributes: well-defined muscles, discernible even beneath the suit jacket; dirty-blond hair long enough on the top to sink her hands into, but clipped super short on the sides; glacial eyes with sandy lashes; and facial hair, the same dirty blond, not quite perfectly trimmed, giving him a rough-and-ready look. All in all, he looked like a man capable of class but ready to go bare knuckle if need be.

It was all quite exciting, really. Except he was probably ten years older than her, barely smiled and was *all* about the job. Pity.

Ah well, no need to be disappointed; she was going to be busy day and night during the trip and a distraction was not what she needed. Still, he'd smiled at her once, and it might be nice if she were able to make him do that again before they headed back home.

She admired his ability to sleep. She'd never been able to sleep while flying; she was a nervous flier though she hid it well, as frequent travel was a thing with her family. The single glass of wine calmed her nerves a little, and she chose to work so she could focus on something other than the fact they were thirty-odd-thousand feet in the air.

Charlotte looked over at Jacob again. He certainly looked capable enough. She'd had qualms about him going everywhere with her, including parties and galas. She didn't want people to know she had a bodyguard, and it occurred to her, as she looked at his relaxed face, that he could certainly pass as her date.

She tapped her fingers on the keyboard. Did she want that, though? It would invite a level of speculation, and the family had already found itself in the tabloids recently. She could just see the headline now. "Who is Charlotte's mystery man?" And then some salacious speculation with no basis at all in fact.

Annoyed, she opened an email from a saved folder and frowned.

New York is the city that never sleeps. You shouldn't either. #sleepwithoneeyeopen

The messages frustrated her. So far Aurora's IT department hadn't been able to trace the source, and Charlotte was sure it wasn't anything too serious. She'd grown up in the spotlight, and knew that hate mail came with the territory from time to time. This was the third message she'd received in the last two months, but nothing had happened. Nothing personal. She'd been outvoted on the protection front, though, with her sister, Bella, being the only one to think she should be able to decide for herself. The trip was only a little over a week. She could deal.

So she closed the email and opened her calendar for the week. This was the perfect quiet time to make any adjustments to her itinerary that needed to be made. And when they landed, they would make their way to Aurora Inc.'s apartment, where she would finally sleep and wake up ready to take on New York.

Jacob wondered how Charlotte could still look so fresh and bright after being up for the whole flight. He'd slept over an hour on the plane, and when he woke she was still typing away on her laptop. Now they were in a cab heading to the Aurora Inc. apartment.

"Do you ever sleep?" he asked, looking over at her.

"Oh, of course." She smiled at him. "I just don't sleep on planes. Once we get settled, I plan to sink into my bed and sleep all morning." She lifted an eyebrow. "You should, too. You only slept an hour."

"I'm used to going without sleep," he replied, looking away and out the window. The city was bright even though the sky was dark.

"And I'm not?" Charlotte laughed a little. "Clearly you've not seen me the night before a major PR push. Coffee and chocolate are my fuel and I go, go, go."

He could just imagine. She seemed full of…

youthful energy. His youthful energy was long gone. Maybe it had just disappeared bit by bit, along with his innocence and optimism. All his life he'd made a living counting on humanity being horrible.

Energy, innocence, optimism…he knew exactly where he'd lost them. He was just fooling himself to think they'd been chipped away in increments. He'd left them in South America. And with one woman, in particular.

He shouldn't resent Charlotte's charmed life. Of course, he would never want her to experience or see what he had. And while her concerns might seem trivial to him, he shouldn't judge. After all, he'd spent half his life working to keep the dark underbelly of society at bay precisely so no one had to ever see the things he'd seen.

Her life was very different, and he didn't fit there. But his job required him to be a chameleon. He'd grown up in scruffy jeans and T-shirts, worn trainers and caps. This week he'd don designer suits and look absolutely like he belonged.

The cab pulled up outside a gray stone building. Charlotte handed over a credit card while Jacob got out and scanned the area, shivering against the February cold. It had a bite to it that seemed to go right through his wool coat and into his skin, and a few snowflakes flitted in the air. The cabbie popped the trunk and Jacob lifted it to retrieve their bags. He had one small rolling case and a garment bag. Charlotte, on the other hand, had her carry-on bag and laptop, and then two large suitcases. She was definitely not a "pack light" kind of woman, but then, she was a Pemberton. Her job required she never be photographed in the same dress twice.

The doorman opened the door and they stepped into the warm lobby. Jacob made his living guarding VIPs, so the opulence wasn't a surprise. It was the kind of space that had nothing to prove; it was expensive but not ostentatious, a quiet sort of wealth in glass, brass and marble. The elevator was huge and nearly silent as they made their way up to the apartment.

He wheeled his suitcase and one of hers into the foyer of the apartment and paused. "Welcome home?" he asked, looking over at her.

"I guess." She sighed. "Would it strike you as strange that I wish this place was smaller and more…cozy?"

It did, but he understood. The foyer was bigger than his living room at home, and that was saying something. They walked through into the main area. It was done in mostly white, with accents in pale green and tan. It was…perfect. Show-home perfect. A vase of white lilies sat on a glass table and the perfumed scent filled the air. The windows provided a dim view of Central Park; he turned his head to the left and thought he could make out the Met, though the snow was coming down harder than it had been only minutes before.

A deep sigh came from behind him, and he turned to find Charlotte standing in the middle of the floor, looking a bit lost.

"Are you all right?"

She nodded, gave a small smile. "Yes. But now that I'm here, I've run out of steam. I think I need to sleep."

"Let me check the other rooms first," Jacob said, slightly annoyed when Charlotte laughed.

"Seriously? I promise no one has been in the apartment and we're perfectly safe. My mother hired you as a precaution. I'm really not in any danger."

"I still have a job to do. Stay put."

He left her in the living room and checked the other rooms—a dining room with a table for eight, a powder room, a massive kitchen that gleamed with stainless steel appliances and two huge bedrooms, each with their own en suite bathroom. Everything was fine, and he went back out to the living room.

Charlotte had sat on the sofa, and her eyes

were closed as she breathed deeply. He'd been maybe five minutes, but she was sound asleep.

Did he leave her there? He needed sleep, too, and had no idea which room was meant to be his, though he could sleep in a chair and have no problem. He knelt before her, looking into her peaceful face, and his heart gave a heavy thump. She was beautiful, there was no denying that. And maybe she was pampered but so far she didn't act spoiled, which was to her credit. He'd read the messages sent to her. Mildly threatening, but not to be discounted.

Maybe she seemed like a spoiled princess, but someone wasn't happy with her. It should be an easy assignment, but he would still be doing his job to the letter.

He reached out and touched her upper arm. "Miss Pemberton."

She snuffled and burrowed deeper into the sofa.

"Miss Pemberton," he said, more firmly. Still nothing, and he gave her arm a little shake. "Charlotte."

Her eyes opened and she blinked, confusion clearing as she looked into his face. "I fell asleep."

"Yes, you did. I thought you'd be more comfortable in your room. I just don't know which one that is."

"Oh. Right. And you'd probably like to sleep, as well." She yawned and then sat up, lifting her arms and stretching a bit. The way she moved her body was languorous and sensual, and Jacob sat back on his heels a bit.

This would be much easier if she were a fifty-something man with a paunch and a bald spot. Oh, he'd be professional, but the attraction he felt was a pain in his ass.

"Come on, then. I'll show you your room first."

She led him down the hall and gestured to the first room. "This one is yours. I've always liked the other one better."

Either one suited him fine. The room was more like a suite than a simple bedroom. There was a small sofa and chair and a coffee table, where another bouquet of fresh flowers sat. The bed was king-size and covered with a gold-and-green brocade spread, the green the same deep color as the upholstery on the sofa and chair. He didn't have to go to the window to know that he had a terrific view of the park. "Wow," he said quietly. "This is very nice."

"What did you think, I was going to make you sleep in the closet?"

"No, of course not."

"Your job is VIP security. Surely this isn't a novelty."

"Usually my accommodations are a few steps up from a closet. Not my own suite."

She leaned against the doorframe. "Well, it's either feast or famine. We don't have anything in the midrange here at Hotel Aurora."

He appreciated her sense of humor, especially since she could find humor when she had to be exhausted. "Sorry. Anyway, thank you. I'll be more than comfortable here."

She nodded toward another door. "Your bathroom is in there. There's a shower and a jetted tub if you're cramped up from sitting in the plane." Her gaze ran from his toes up to his eyes. "You're a bit tall to be jammed into those seats. Even the first-class ones."

He was six three. And apparently she had noticed, because as he held her gaze, her cheeks turned a charming shade of pink.

She pushed away from the doorframe. "Right. I'm next door. I'll be drawing the curtains and sleeping until about noon. I have a meeting here at three with my assistant, who arrived a few days ago."

"She's not staying here?"

"She's staying at the hotel with the rest of the staff."

Interesting. "I'll see you at noon, then."

Charlotte disappeared from the doorway and he heard her go inside her room and shut the door. A few minutes later, he heard the muffled sound of the shower running, and tried not to think of her long legs and slight curves under the hot spray. He wasn't a monk, for God's sake. He could appreciate a beautiful woman and still keep his head for the job.

And to prove it, he opened up his bag, plugged in his laptop and retrieved his file on Charlotte's assistant, Amelie. Once he'd read it over twice, he was satisfied. He stripped off his suit, jumped in the shower and then crawled into the plush bed.

It was heaven. And if he was in it alone, it was no more than he deserved. It was his last thought before drifting off to sleep.

CHAPTER TWO

CHARLOTTE CHOPPED FRESH strawberries and dumped them over a bowl of yogurt. She wasn't up for a full meal right now; her internal clock was all messed up with the time difference. She had coffee brewing in the French press, and she looked at the blueberry muffins and turned up her nose. American muffins were so…cakey. And also seemed too heavy right now.

But she was ready to meet with Amelie and go over details. Amelie was her boots on the ground and she was incredibly good at her job. They'd go over the itinerary, any new invitations, interview requests and coverage for Aurora's show. Then there was the guest list for the party Charlotte was hosting at the Waldorf. There were always last-minute additions.

It was all terribly exciting. She'd been along for the trip twice, but both times her mother had been in charge and Charlotte had ridden on her coattails. Charlotte was thrilled to have this chance, bodyguard or not. She had always been Aurora Germain's daughter or William's twin sister or the youngest daughter. Sometimes she wanted to be herself, and recognized for her own achievements and not anyone else's.

Being a part of Aurora Inc.'s empire meant there were limitations to that desire. And she wouldn't leave the company or the family. But she desperately wanted to put her own stamp on something. Create her own legitimacy.

It wouldn't happen overnight, but this trip was a good start.

Her stomach growled and she turned her attention back to her light meal. Yesterday the housekeeper had stocked the fridge and pantry in anticipation of Charlotte's arrival. Her favorite Icelandic yogurt and fresh berries were the perfect pick-me-up. She hadn't seen or heard anything from her bodyguard, which she counted as a blessing. Maybe he was still sleeping. Either way, it felt odd having a stranger in the apartment.

After the yogurt was gone, she poured her coffee and set up her laptop and a few files on the dining room table. The doorbell rang, and before she could go to the door and open it herself, Jacob strode past the kitchen to the foyer.

So he was up.

He stepped back into the kitchen with their

guest, Amelie, who sported a raised eyebrow and an amused expression, and Jacob frowning. Again.

"Did the doorman call up and announce Ms. Beauchamp's arrival?"

"No, of course not."

"He's supposed to. It's part of the security measures."

"It's just Amelie." She gave a little laugh and held out a cup. "Coffee?"

"Oui," Amelie answered. "Do you have to ask?"

Jacob was still standing and scowling, and Charlotte sighed. "What?"

"It was Amelie this time. But we do not want strangers having access to this apartment. I'll have to speak to the door staff to make sure this doesn't happen again."

"Jacob, it's fine."

He bristled. "Let me do my job, okay?"

"Fine. If you want coffee, fix it yourself. It sounds as though you could use a shot of caffeine."

She led Amelie into the dining room, and gestured to the empty chair. "Sorry about that. Apparently he goes everywhere I go."

Amelie's blue eyes darkened with worry. "But why? Is something going on I should know about?"

Charlotte debated how much to tell her assistant and her staff in general. She didn't want to scare her, and didn't want staff gossip, either. As much as she trusted her people, rumors did get out. At the same time, it wasn't fair to leave her next-in-command in the dark.

"Do you remember the strange letter I got last fall?"

"The one that said you were a viper and that your day would come? Of course. It was not only odd, but vicious."

"It wasn't the only one. I haven't said anything because nothing has escalated, really. No real threats, nothing violent. But Maman would only let me take point on this trip if I agreed to a bodyguard, so there you have it. Jacob Wolfe, who is going to be a thorn in my side until I get back to Paris."

Amelie took a sip of her coffee and lowered her voice. "I don't know, Charlotte. He's terribly good-looking."

She wasn't wrong, and it wasn't like Charlotte hadn't noticed. Even standing in the kitchen with a scowl on his face, he cut an impressive figure. He'd ditched the suit and now wore jeans and a sweater, the first fitting his long legs and fine butt perfectly and the second managing to make his shoulders look even more forbidding. His hair was rumpled as if he'd run his fingers through it, and his eyes had been icy fire as he'd told her to let him do his job.

He was an intense man. She kind of liked it, not that she'd admit such a thing. Besides, she had to focus on the job at hand. "Well, looks aren't everything," she responded. "Now, let's look at the schedule. You can bring me up to date with the various preparations, and we can decide what I need for my own appearances. I'm particularly nervous about the interview with *Vogue*."

Amelie opened her case and took out her laptop, and as she set it up, Charlotte heard noises coming from the kitchen. She really should have been more gracious and fixed him a coffee. Or told him to help himself to the food in the fridge. Instead she'd put her nose in the air.

Charlotte swallowed tightly as she recalled the letter that had accused her of being a "stuck-up bitch." Was she? Or was she just trying to find her way and sometimes failing?

"Charlotte?" Amelie's voice cut into her thoughts. "What do you think about the interview with *Vogue* tomorrow?"

"Oh. Right." Charlotte shook her head and reminded herself to focus on the job at hand. She couldn't let herself be distracted. "Let's go over the details again."

They spent three hours and drank tons more

coffee before they were through it all. Aurora's show wasn't until Wednesday, at Spring Studios, and there was already a team in place preparing for that. All Charlotte had to do was be the face of the company, the representative on the ground if anything went wrong, and show up at all the sparkling engagements. It sounded easy, but she felt a lot of pressure to do her mother and the company proud. To look her best. To be effervescent and lovely and smart in the interviews. To be herself and yet be all things Aurora. The balancing act was sometimes tough to execute.

The interview prep was the biggest thing. She had a document that was fifty pages long of talking points and highlights of each division's key initiatives. When six o'clock arrived, Amelie looked at her phone and then at Charlotte.

Charlotte grinned; she recognized that look. "Dinner plans?"

"At seven thirty."

"And you need to change."

Amelie smiled back, her eyes twinkling. "Something like that."

"Go, we've covered lots of ground this afternoon. We'll pick you up in the morning, so we can be in Tribeca at eight thirty." Charlotte shuddered. That sounded so early, though with the jet lag she'd probably be up at four in the morning anyway.

"Perfect. See you then." Then Amelie leaned over and murmured, "I suppose you're bringing your Mr. Wolfe with you?"

Heat rushed into Charlotte's cheeks. "He's not my Mr. Wolfe. And yes. This week, he goes where I go."

Amelie's eyes twinkled again and Charlotte laughed. "Go, or you'll be late."

She heard Amelie wish Jacob a good evening, and his lower response. The deepness of his voice set something off in her belly, something unexpected and a bit wicked. Ugh, she hadn't had time for romance in ages, and most would be surprised how quiet her social life was. Now she was shacked up with Jacob for a week and she'd need to keep it totally professional.

That didn't mean she was blind and didn't have an imagination, though. And not for the first time in her life, she knew her imagination had the potential to get her into trouble.

Jacob saw Amelie to the door and then let out a breath when he closed it behind her. He was alone with Charlotte now, and while he had always been a consummate professional, he'd also never had a client so...*lovely*. It seemed an innocuous word, but it suited her. He could have said *beautiful* or *stunning*, but it wasn't just her looks. Even when she was a little on the annoyed side of things, there was a gentleness to her that he liked. Not to be mistaken for weakness, though. He was good at reading people, and he knew instinctively that Charlotte might have an innate sweetness, but she knew her mind and knew how to get things done. He was sure she could tell off any of his men and they'd all say, "Aw, thanks, love."

He smiled a little at that. She was lovely, and not to be underestimated. He'd caught bits and pieces of her conversation with Amelie and very quickly understood that this week wasn't about being a social butterfly, but representing a multinational company during one of the biggest weeks of the year.

So what if fashion wasn't his thing? Clearly it was big business, and he respected that.

She was still in the dining room, clicking away on her laptop, so he figured he might as well start some dinner. The fridge was well stocked, and he was surprised to find some of his favorites among the offerings. Aurora had been very thorough, hadn't they? He took out some chicken and vegetables and started making a simple stir-fry.

He popped his head into the dining room and asked, "You're not vegetarian, are you?"

She looked up, through her glasses that made her seem damned sexy. "What? Oh, no, I'm not. I don't eat much red meat, but truthfully I'll eat almost anything."

"Music to my ears. Dinner in twenty minutes."

"Jacob, you don't have to cook—"

"I don't mind. Not much else to do when we're here. Besides, I'm hungry." He flashed her a smile and then dipped back into the kitchen.

Cooking was something he knew how to do and he enjoyed. His mother had died when he was twelve, leaving him with his dad, a Met police officer. The two of them had learned to cook together, first simple stuff, and then more involved. He could make a wicked cottage pie, and a more than passable butter chicken. For years he'd eaten in mess halls and MREs in the field, but at home he liked indulging in cooking for himself.

A stir-fry? He could do that with his eyes closed.

The scents of garlic and ginger wafted up as he went to work chopping peppers and mushrooms. He found broccoli in the crisper and a bag of bean sprouts. As the chicken sizzled, he searched the pantry for what he needed to make a simple sauce, and then a bag of rice and a steamer. Perfect. It was all on the go when Charlotte finally stepped inside the room.

"That smells amazing."

He looked up and smiled. "I can cook. Surprised?"

"To be honest? Yes."

"I was brought up by a single dad. We either had to learn to cook, starve, or eat ramen for the rest of our lives. We picked cooking."

She moved farther into the room while he stirred the mixture in the stir-fry pan. "A single dad, huh?"

"And a police officer. Lots of shift work." He remembered back to the early days when they'd been alone, trying to manage the simplest things while dealing with their grief and loneliness, as a husband and as a child. "My mum died when I was twelve. My dad said we were going to be a team and that we had to rely on each other. And so we did." He shrugged and reached for the sauce he'd mixed together. "It set me up well for the SAS. If you don't operate as a team, you're screwed."

Charlotte picked up a stray piece of red pepper and nibbled on it. "And you left the military because…"

It wasn't an easy question to answer. He'd left at age thirty-three, still young. The wound to his leg had set him back, but he could have resumed. After that last mission, he'd lost the taste for it. He'd lost his faith—in himself, in a lot of things. His heart had told him to walk away. His dad had told him to find a way to use his skills so he could pay his rent. Now he more than paid his rent. He ran an agency with over fifty operatives worldwide and an exclusive clientele, and he was expanding every day.

He'd hesitated too long and Charlotte looked away. "Forget I asked. It's none of my business."

"The most important thing for you to know," he said, stirring the vegetables again, "is that I'm very good at what I do."

"Including cooking." She looked up again and caught his eye, and her lips quirked a little, hinting at teasing.

"Including cooking." He tried a smile back, but when they smiled at each other something happened. It wasn't just polite. It felt as though it fed this strange connection between them. And being friends with a client wasn't a good idea, either.

He poured the sauce over the stir-fry and checked the steamer. "This is almost done, if you want to grab a few bowls."

"All right."

She got out dishes and cutlery and glasses and put them on a counter with barstools on the other side, rather than in the formal dining room. He was glad about that. As he spooned rice into two bowls, Charlotte filled glasses with iced water from the fridge dispenser. He was surprised. No wine? No cocktails? Maybe he was misreading Charlotte. Maybe she was not as high maintenance as he'd originally thought.

They sat together and Charlotte was the first to dig in.

"This is delicious." She fanned her mouth. "And hot." The words were slightly muffled.

He laughed, then made a show of scooping up some food and blowing on it before putting it in his mouth.

Charlotte reached for her water and took a substantial sip. "So, about tomorrow. I told Amelie we'd pick her up at her hotel. I'm thinking right around eight, shortly after. The shows start at nine and even with weekend traffic being lighter, that doesn't give us much of a buffer."

"I'll contact our driver and make sure everything's arranged."

"I have an interview with *Vogue* at one thirty. We'll be doing lunch."

"I saw that in your schedule." He ate more of the stir-fry and his stomach gurgled in approval. He hadn't eaten all day. This was definitely hitting the spot.

Charlotte went quiet for a few minutes and

he finally looked over at her. She was picking at her food, a slight frown marring her smooth face. "What's wrong? Did I put something in you don't like?"

She looked up, her eyes wide. "Oh, no! This is delicious. I just… Okay, so here's the thing. I don't really want people to know I have a bodyguard, and I'm not sure how else to explain your presence, unless…"

Her cheeks turned pink.

Ah.

"You can say I'm your driver."

"My driver wouldn't sit next to me at a show."

"Distant cousin?"

She sent him a withering look and he laughed. "I see where you're going. People are going to think I'm your date. And a serious one, because I'll be everywhere you are."

"If you're my bodyguard, they'll ask why. If you're my date, they'll ask who. And then why."

"Why do you have to explain anything at all?"

She paused. "I don't. You know, sometimes I really do have to balance which is better. No response or stepping up and controlling the narrative. I'm one hundred percent sure, though, that sometime in the next week, a photographer will get a shot and the question of your identity will be out there. To be honest, that's a big reason why I fought against having you along at all. Our family is just getting over one scandal."

Jacob sat back a bit and grinned. "Oh, so I'd be a scandal? Exciting."

She rolled her eyes. "Don't sound like you'd enjoy it. You'd hate it. The paparazzi are relentless."

And she had to deal with it every day in her line of work. Fame and success came with a price, he supposed. And as much as he joked about being a scandal, he knew she was right. He wouldn't like it. He was a private man used to being in the background and that was how he wanted it to stay.

"If push comes to shove, you can simply say I'm a family friend who happens to be in town." He understood why she wouldn't want to pretend he was her date. He wasn't exactly up to Pemberton standards. There was absolutely no blue blood in his family tree at all.

"Please understand, it's not that I'd be ashamed or anything." Her cheeks colored again. "You're a really good-looking guy, and…" Her voice trailed off, as if she didn't know what to say next.

"I get it, so don't worry. I'm your employee."

"No, that's not it at all!" She put down her fork with a clatter. "It's more… It's not about you at all. It's the speculation I hate. My brothers were just dragged through the tabloids. I don't want to do the same to the family or the company." She sighed. "I'm in PR and, no matter how I spin this, I see someone digging and finding out you're private protection and fabricating some wild story."

He met her gaze squarely. "I always say when in doubt, go with the truth. I'm private security for the trip. And if it doesn't come up at all, don't worry about it. A good rule of thumb is to only explain what you must."

She let out a sigh and her shoulders relaxed. "All right. That's what we'll do, then."

"Tomorrow," he added, "we can look at alternatives. I might not have to sit beside you, for example. I can be nearby at the restaurant where you're doing your interview."

"I've restricted most of my activities to ones that are not open to the public," she admitted. "Thinking it would help."

He'd made the recommendation. "I know. It does help."

"I really don't think anyone wants to hurt me, Jacob. This is so unnecessary."

She looked so unhappy that he took pity on her. "Your family cares about you and wants you safe. Not everyone has that, Charlotte. Just look at it that way."

She nodded and picked at her dinner. "I know

that. Sometimes we fight like cats and dogs, but in the end, we all love each other very much."

"All right, then. Let me clean up this mess and you can do whatever it is you need to do tonight. I see there's a gym in the building. I'd like to work out in the morning, but it'll be early. Just please don't leave the building without me, all right?"

She nodded. "All right."

CHAPTER THREE

WHEN CHARLOTTE WOKE up at five thirty, she tiptoed out of her room to see if Jacob was up. His bedroom door was open, and his bed neatly made. A quick check of the rest of the apartment told her he was at the building's gym.

Her stomach growled.

It was ridiculous how she could even be hungry after last night's dinner. Jacob was indeed a good cook, and the spicy-sweet stir-fry had hit the spot. Now that she'd somewhat got her body back on a schedule—even though it was much later in Paris—she was craving something entirely different, and something she got only when she was in New York. Bagels. And very possibly blintzes.

Except Jacob had told her, in no uncertain terms, that she wasn't to leave the apartment.

This whole thing was dumb. Someone had sent her a few emails and she couldn't go out for bagels? She didn't have security in Paris, so why here? The deli was maybe a five-minute walk. She could be there and back before Jacob even knew she'd been gone.

She hurried into a pair of yoga pants, put on a hoodie over her pajama tank and hoped the weather wasn't too cold. At the door, she paused again, knowing she was going against Jacob's orders. And yet he'd already agreed to loosen things a bit during the runway shows. She set her chin and pulled a knitted hat over her head. Ten minutes. That was all she'd be gone, and then she'd be back with breakfast, and they could get on with their day.

The weather had warmed slightly from the previous day, but the wind still held a bite that cut through her hoodie and sliced into her skin. She hurried down the street feeling as if she were in a wind tunnel, then turned left and had a few moments of respite. Then, there it was. A plain, ordinary deli that looked like a thousand other delis in New York. She grinned. She loved this city. It was energetic and brash and unapologetic, with such a different feel from any other city in the world. She stepped inside the door, out of the cold, and let the warmth seep in.

Even at 6:00 a.m. the foot traffic was brisk. Half the seats were full and there was a line about six deep for takeaway bagels. When it was her turn, she ordered a half dozen with a variety of cream cheeses and a small bit of lox, just in case Jacob liked it. Then cheese blintzes, her personal favorite, because she had a sweet tooth and couldn't resist the blueberry compote that came with them. Finally she ordered a coffee, because the walk back was surely going to be just as cold.

She was humming something rather tunelessly when she opened the door to the apartment and came face-to-face with an irate Jacob.

Busted.

His eyes were that flinty gray that she was quickly coming to understand meant he was displeased. Displeased was putting it mildly. A tick in his jaw told her he was furious.

"You left the apartment. After I explicitly told you not to."

She tried a disarming smile and lifted the paper bag. "You were working out. I got bagels."

The fire in his eyes made her lower her arm, because he looked like he wanted to rip the bag from her fingers and throw it across the room. He didn't, though. He remained perfectly steady. She wasn't afraid of his anger, she realized. It was his job to protect her. She lifted her chin. "I was gone ten minutes. Maybe fifteen. There was a small line. And look! Nothing happened."

He let out a slow breath. It appeared as if he was counting to ten.

When he finally spoke, his voice was measured, but with a hard edge that told her he was, indeed, furious with her. "Since I can't trust you to follow my instructions, now I'm going to be on your six every damned minute. And I'm not giving up my workouts while I'm here, so that means tomorrow morning you're up at five and going to the gym with me."

Her mouth dropped open. Five a.m. gym times were Bella's thing, not hers. She preferred an extra hour or so of sleep, and then coffee. Lots of coffee.

"You seem to be forgetting that you work for me, not the other way around."

He smiled then, and she wondered if she was being forgiven. "No, love. I work for your mother. I'll be happy to send her a report after the first twenty-four hours letting her know that we didn't even make it one day without you going off on your own."

"You're going to tell on me to my mother."

"I'm obligated to, as per my contract."

He was immovable. She knew that as sure as she knew she was breathing. She realized he'd given her a test and she'd failed spectacularly because she'd thought a quick trip out wouldn't hurt. And it hadn't! But it did have consequences. Jacob Wolfe was now going to be with her all the time.

"The press will pick up on this for sure. You truly don't have to be on me like…like a barnacle."

He stepped back and his shoulders relaxed. "Respectfully, that sounds like a you problem. And since you're running PR, it shouldn't be that hard to spin."

"You're insufferable!"

He shrugged. "I've definitely been called worse." He looked down at his watch. "And your time would be better spent getting ready and having one of those bagels if you actually eat breakfast. We're leaving at eight ten sharp."

She glared at him. He really could not be moved. Then again, he was former SAS. She supposed he'd stared down people a lot tougher than her.

She took the bag to the counter, put all the blintzes on a plate, took the compote, a napkin and a fork and knife, glared at him, and marched to her room.

He couldn't have any of the good pastries. And fine. She'd get dressed and they'd do their thing and she'd ignore him. That was what he wanted anyway, wasn't it?

She sat at the small table in her room and ate every single blintz, determined to enjoy every last bite. When she was done she instantly regretted it; it was too much food and definitely too much pastry and now she had to dress for the day and—worse—for the cameras. She pulled out the outfit for today and sighed. If she had any bloating at all she was going to be hugely uncomfortable. But she had gone over all her wardrobe choices with Amelie as well as the head stylist at Aurora. This was perfect for her interview today, in Aurora colors, and so she pulled on the black lace skirt and then added the white blouse with lace accents, a small peplum that accented her trim waist, and a scoop neckline that was just daring enough to show the smallest shadow of cleavage.

The skirt felt tight, dammit.

Then it was the shoes, classic black stilettos that would put her maybe two inches shorter than Jacob. Not that she cared.

She hoped he realized that yesterday's jeans and sweater wasn't going to cut it when they were in public.

Her makeup regime was down to a science. She sat at the makeup table with the beautiful lighting and began, taking comfort in the steps. Oddly enough, it soothed her. She never went in for dramatic makeup. Oh, for evening events she sometimes went for a bolder eye or lip, but most days she opted for something low-key and classic. She sorted through her lip colors and found the one they'd picked out for the shoot. She'd take a kit with her to freshen her look before the interview. No photos from the interview would be published without her signing off on them first, so she wasn't overly worried.

The only thing she was remotely worried about this morning was Jacob. She'd angered him and now there were consequences. She felt like a chastised child, but had to push those feelings away. They weren't…helpful. Instead she had to deal with what was right in front of her.

Jacob tried to tune out whatever Amelie and Charlotte were talking about and focused instead on the day's itinerary. Their driver wound his way through the streets to Tribeca, where they'd take in a few of the shows and then Charlotte would leave for her interview. Every night there were parties, and tonight was no exception. He glanced over at Charlotte and pondered. He'd never heard any rumors of her being a party girl, but that didn't mean much. Tonight he'd stick close to her side and hope he didn't end up being the babysitter he'd first feared. Today's bagel incident didn't give him much hope in that regard. She definitely didn't like to be told what to do.

When they arrived, Jacob got out and held

the door, and then Amelie gave a small wave and disappeared.

"Where's she going?"

"Oh, here and there. She'll see most of the shows today, network… She has her own seating."

"Not with you?"

Charlotte looked up at him. "No. You get her VIP seat."

He felt momentarily guilty about it, since clearly this was important to Amelie, too. But then, if Charlotte hadn't ignored his directions, he might have compromised.

"Lucky me." He supposed he'd have to sit next to her and look at least a little bit interested. It might be the toughest part of this job.

Charlotte huffed out a sigh. "Are you going to be this annoying all the time?"

"Sorry," he said brusquely. "My job isn't to make conversation. I'll be quiet."

And then he was, and he suspected that drove her even crazier.

Charlotte stopped several times to say hello, and the few times questioning glances were sent Jacob's way, she simply introduced him as Jacob, in keeping with the decision to not offer more information than necessary. He dutifully smiled and then kept eyes on the entire room as she circulated, slowly making her way toward their seats, which he realized were right in the front row. The closer they got, the more people he recognized. Like famous actresses and… He blinked and tried not to stare. A former president's daughter. One he'd actually met a few years earlier while providing security for a UK dignitary at an event. He doubted she'd recognize him. People didn't tend to, because he was in the background.

Except today. Today he was sitting front and center with Charlotte Pemberton.

She leaned over and whispered, "If you feel conspicuous, you can always trade with Amelie."

He turned his head and met her eyes, their heads close together. "I'm fine here. Then I know where you are."

She sat back and pasted on a generic smile that belied her annoyance. "You're still angry about this morning."

"No. I'm just doing my job, remember?"

She crossed her legs and his mouth went dry. It was impossible to ignore her long legs. She was so damned classy. The lace skirt came to just below her knee, utterly modest, but fit every curve perfectly. She didn't wear any jewelry around her neck, nothing to distract from the neckline of her blouse, and that delectable shadow just above the top button. It was sexy as hell and still, with the ruffly thing at her waist and the lace accents on her sleeves, it was elegant and subdued. Was she? So far he'd seen her working, incessantly tapping on her laptop, and always perfectly dressed. For someone he assumed was a party girl, Charlotte Pemberton was actually a bit…uptight.

And stubborn. He'd seen her pile her plate with pastries and she'd eaten them all. Just to spite him. He smiled to himself, remembering.

"What are you smiling at?"

He lifted his head and looked into her eyes. "Just thinking that this is almost as good as a few weeks in Tenerife."

She opened her mouth to ask him more, but then the show started and conversation came to a halt. Jacob braced himself. All he had to do was sit here and look interested, keep his eye on Charlotte. She was focused intently on the models walking the runway at the moment, and he could see her mind working. Always working.

No, he rather suspected Charlotte wasn't a spoiled party girl at all. If anything, he thought she might be a bit of a workaholic. And that made them more alike than she knew.

His impression of her was reinforced several times during the day. There were two hours of shows, then they exited, just the two of them, and went to the car to be transported to a restaurant for the interview. He watched, fascinated, as Charlotte pulled out a bag full of cosmetics and a lighted mirror, which she handed to him to hold.

"You're going to fix your makeup in a moving car," he said, a bit amazed.

"Lips and eyes only get done while we're stopped," she said, and then grinned. "Though I always have a horrible premonition I'm going to do that and then end up looking like Bridget Jones when she goes to the law dinner do."

"I'm not familiar."

"No, I suppose not. It's a movie. Well, based on a book. Anyway, poor Bridget, she's awkward as ass and a total fish out of water going to her boyfriend's work thing, and she does her makeup in the taxi and goes in looking red as a fire hydrant."

All this time Charlotte was blotting her face with some sort of sponge. They stopped at a light and she whipped out her lipstick. A few swipes and her lips were plump and pink again…perfect. His gaze dropped to them and he swallowed tightly. It wouldn't do to be attracted to her, would it? Total dereliction of his duty… Well, if he acted on it. Which he wouldn't. Getting involved on a mission could have dire consequences, as he well knew. Even now, the twinge of guilt darted through him, leaving the bitter taste of regret in his mouth.

He had no idea what movie she was talking about, but it clearly amused her, and her eyes twinkled at him over the rim of the mirror, lightening his dark thoughts. "Do I look all right?"

"You'll do," he answered, looking away. She wasn't all right; she was perfect. He was surprised when she laughed.

"High praise indeed."

"Sorry." He let his gaze catch hers. "You're a beautiful woman, Charlotte, with or without makeup." He'd seen her without this morning and that same punch-to-the-gut feeling had happened, even when he'd been furious. "So don't worry about the interview."

Her lips dropped open a little in surprise. "Thank you. For the compliment and the boost of confidence. Apparently you're more than a simple bodyguard. You're the cheerleading section, too."

He'd never been called that before. At least not in this job. He snorted a little at the idea and her lips curved in a smile, while the air in the car seemed to rise a good ten degrees.

They arrived at their destination, some trendy place in Hell's Kitchen he'd never heard

of, and once more he got out and held the door
for her. "Thank you, Jacob," she said smoothly,
and the personal spark in her eye was gone.
She was in full work mode again. And it got
him thinking.

Once inside he did a quick perusal and then
grabbed a stool at the bar while Charlotte met
with the journalist. It seemed they already knew
each other, and they settled into easy conversation over lunchtime drinks.

Jacob ordered iced water.

A while later, he saw Charlotte and the other
woman ordering lunch, and he realized they
were going to be here awhile. His tastes were
simple, so he ordered something for himself, the
simplest thing he could find on the menu that
didn't have a description four lines long. When
it came, he settled the bill, not wanting to leave
it to Charlotte. He'd simply expense it, with anything else required above his salary this week.
He'd finished and was sipping on another glass
of water when the meeting seemed to be winding up. It had been nearly two hours since they
walked in the door.

Charlotte rose, retrieved her coat, and she and
the other woman exchanged a cheek kiss before
going on their way. All the while that serene,
lovely smile was on Charlotte's lips. Jacob got

up from his stool and met her near the door. "Ready to go?"

"Yes. Back to the shows. There are two more I need to go to today."

Two more? Jacob wouldn't say it out loud, but he didn't get fashion. No one he knew would be caught dead wearing any of those things in public.

"You're the boss," he said gamely, and took her elbow as they stepped out into the sunny but chilly February air.

Everything changed once they were back in the car, though. Charlotte wilted and closed her eyes as she leaned back against the seat. "*Mon Dieu*, that was exhausting."

"You looked like you were having a nice time." Jacob frowned. There'd been nothing but smiles during the interview.

"You think that was real? I mean, Lauralea is nice enough, and does a good job, but the whole time I was measuring every answer, considering my body language, making sure I didn't get salad dressing on my blouse. Thank God there were no pictures today, which I thought there would be. But I did invite her to the Aurora party on Wednesday. She'll bring a photographer, I'm sure."

"You looked completely at ease," he assured her, amazed.

"I've had years of practice." She opened her small handbag and took out a protein bar. "I also ate about thirty calories worth of salad. I'm starving."

He was going to say something about the morning pastries, but decided against it. No need bringing up that argument again. "If I'd known I'd have snuck out a takeaway bag," he said, truly sorry it had been a tough few hours. "Let me know if you need me to next time. I had some sort of hanger steak thing that was delicious."

Her stomach growled and she chuckled wearily. "It's mean of you to bring it up."

"Sorry."

She ate the protein bar and then leaned her head back on the cushioned seat with a sigh.

"Are you really all right?"

She opened one eye and nodded. "Of course. With this kind of event, I'm 'on' all the time. Being in the car? It gives me a chance to regroup and recharge. And this week… It's a little more hectic than my usual schedule."

"Very nonstop," he agreed. "You're right to take some quiet time. In my experience, things go hinky when people get overtired and overwhelmed."

"Like when?" She turned her head, looking genuinely interested.

"Well, there was one instance where my team was sent in to extricate three hostages. We got in just fine. But the three people we went in to rescue were so tired and had so much adrenaline running through them that they really kind of lost it."

"What did you do?" She sat up now, her eyes alight with curiosity.

He grinned at her. "Threatened to shoot all three if they didn't shut up and do what they were told."

Her eyes widened. "And what happened?"

"They shut up." When she laughed, he smiled. "Point being, you are not in a hostage situation, but you are in danger of being overtired or over-stimulated, and so taking time to decompress is a smart thing to do."

"So you really did all that Special Forces stuff?"

He nodded. "I really did it. For a lot of years. Until…" He hesitated, swallowed, unsure of why he wanted to share any part of himself with her but feeling the need to anyway. "I got injured, and my heart wasn't in it anymore. So I retired."

"There's more to that story, isn't there?"

A lump formed in his throat, another surprise. "There is." But he didn't want to go into that—he'd already blurred the line between professional and personal. He cleared his throat and asked, "What else is on the agenda today?"

Thankfully, she took the hint, and slid back into work mode. "A few more shows, then I have a meeting with the team from Paris who is putting together our show. We have had this planned for weeks, and I had a bit of a practice run in Paris last fall. I trust them to do their job and don't want to overstep. I'm just there if they need anything."

"Because you do PR."

"Because I do PR. And because I have a decent handle on all areas of our business. It's not just our designs on display. All the cosmetics are from Aurora's new Naturel line, and the jewelry, as well." She smiled. "Maman has built an empire."

Jacob pondered that for a few moments. It had to be difficult to be Aurora Germain's child. Aurora had accomplished so much, how could any of the children hope to compete or even just meet expectations?

He looked back at Charlotte. She'd leaned her head against the back of the seat again and closed her eyes. He wondered if she felt the heavy weight of expectation on her shoulders.

Before he could ask her, they were back at Spring Studios for the next round of shows. And as she opened her eyes, he saw the same determined set to her jaw as he had earlier this morning and before her interview.

Charlotte was putting on a show of her own. But how long could she keep it up?

CHAPTER FOUR

IT HAD BEEN a grueling day, Charlotte was still feeling the effects of jet lag, and the last thing she wanted to do was head to a party. But her absence would be noted, and she was determined to give this trip her all, so she took a deep breath and stepped out of the car, grateful for Jacob's hand as she settled on her heels.

She hadn't eaten enough today. Or at least, not since this morning and the sweet pastries, which had only given her a sugar crash later. Now it was nine o'clock and she had maybe three more hours of being "on" before she could go back home and fall into bed.

Jacob offered his elbow, his face unreadable. She was grateful for the support, to be honest. Perhaps it was inappropriate, considering his job, but he was someone to lean on for a few moments, and that was something she didn't often have.

Often? More like never. Charlotte hadn't had

a relationship in three years, after a disastrous breakup with someone she'd imagined was Mr. Right. Mark had proved to be someone other than she thought. A climber, which she couldn't fault. She had no problem with ambition. She did have a problem when people used other people to achieve it, though. She hadn't realized he'd been using the same tactics on other women, too, until the gossip had reached her ears. His attempts at placating her and justifying his actions had made her angry as well as broke her heart.

She could count the actual dates she'd had since on one hand. Her twin brother, William, told her she worked too hard. She wasn't sure he was wrong, but she also didn't see another way. Her work? It never let her down.

Cameras flashed as they entered the Mandarin Oriental. She looked over at Jacob and saw that his jaw was set; she was sure he wasn't used to the cameras and attention. Normally he'd be a few steps behind, in the background, wouldn't he? And he could have been tonight, except he'd offered her his arm. Why?

Once inside they made their way to the party, and Charlotte let go of his arm. "Doing better?" he asked quietly.

"I was fine before," she replied, but her heart fluttered a little. What had he noticed? And why?

"You're exhausted." He angled her a sideways look. "You're jet-lagged and you've been going for well over twelve hours now on a handful of blintzes and a protein bar."

She wasn't sure if she should be touched or annoyed at his attention. "I didn't realize that watching my dietary habits was part of your job description."

He snorted. "It's not. But I notice things anyway." He looked into her eyes. "In my line of work, observation is key."

"You'll notice a lot tonight," she said, her stomach in knots. "Tons of A-listers here. And there's always Fashion Week drama."

"As long as the drama doesn't involve harming you, I'm good."

Right. Because he was her bodyguard. The protective statement shouldn't feel so comforting, but it did. Charlotte was very used to handling herself, and she knew she could. But she couldn't deny it felt good having a wingman tonight. What he'd said earlier about exhaustion and feeling overwhelmed rang in her ears. Tonight she was both.

She was even happier to have his company when they entered the room that was already packed. Just inside the door, Jacob reached down and tugged on her hand. "I'm sticking close. And you should hydrate. You haven't eaten enough today, but keeping hydrated will help."

"I think I can manage," she said, but knew he was right. She watched as he undid the button on his suit jacket. She was in a black dress, a straight column with simple lines, and a white band across the bodice—the Aurora brand colors. At her ears were the diamonds that her father had given her on her eighteenth birthday. Last fall she'd loaned them to Gabi Baresi, for the night that William proposed. Right now they kept Charlotte anchored. Cedric Pemberton had been a wonderful father and a steadying influence.

She fully expected to see some gorgeous and innovative wardrobe choices tonight. But for her... She wasn't a model. She stuck with what Aurora did best: the red carpet look.

The noise was spectacular. She didn't recognize the singer on stage. He was good, though loud enough one had to shout to talk at all. Within twenty steps she'd stopped six times to greet people with more excitement than she felt, while Jacob tried to keep a neutral expression. She saw him struggle when she introduced him as "my dear friend Jacob," to a recent Oscar winner, who'd worn an Aurora gown to the awards the previous year.

He pressed a glass of water into her hands

and took a drink of his own. "Hydrate," he ordered again, and she obeyed, because the cold water tasted so good. But it wasn't long before she had a champagne glass in her hand. Jacob stayed just behind her, at her hip, still drinking water. Probably because he was on duty.

But she was safe. She knew it. Those emails were nothing, and tonight's party was invitation only. Right now her biggest enemy was fatigue and hunger. And she could make it a few hours.

"I'm going to the ladies' room." She leaned over and tilted her head up so he could hear her. "I'll be fine."

"I'll come with you and wait by the door."

She met his gaze and shook her head. "Please don't. It'll look as though you're…possessive. Like you can't let me go to the bathroom by myself. I promise I'm okay."

"I'll wait for you outside the ballroom doors, then." He offered a compromise and she could live with it. "I can see anyone who goes in or out."

"Jacob…"

"Indulge me, Charlotte. We don't know who sent those emails."

She sighed. "Fine."

It was good to slip out of the crowd for a few moments and head to the slightly quieter ladies' room. She locked herself in a stall and took three minutes to deep-breathe. There were others in the room, and their conversations came and went, and when Charlotte finally felt slightly restored, she flushed the unused toilet and unlocked the door.

At the mirrors she touched up her hair and lipstick, then let out a huge breath and prepared to face the party again.

Outside, wearing a broad smile, was Mark Church, holding two glasses of champagne.

She stopped. Tonight was the first time she'd thought of him in months, and now here he was. "Mark."

"Hello, Charlotte."

Oh, the way he said it was so warm and familiar. It made her remember the good times, but the memories were quickly tainted by the reminder of his betrayals. She'd been young and foolish, but trusting him had taught her a valuable lesson. So she smiled because it made sense to let bygones be bygones. "I didn't realize you'd be here tonight."

"I managed an invitation."

Of course he had. That was how he operated. And now, some of his clients were the highest-paid models in the world. It burned that she had to maintain a cordial relationship, but the truth was, it was good for Aurora to not burn any bridges.

He offered her the glass of champagne. "How about a toast to old times?"

She took it and lifted an eyebrow. "I was twenty-two and very, very green," she said, a veiled way of saying she'd been naive and foolish.

"Maybe we're both older and wiser now?" He smiled his charming smile, and she smiled back. Politely. Thankfully, she felt nothing but regret and relief seeing him now. No lingering attraction, no pain. Just regret that she'd been so gullible and relieved that it was truly behind her. Now if she could just extricate herself gracefully...

She saw Jacob out of the corner of her eye and waved him off with a subtle flick of her hand. He paused, but his eyes never left them. Suddenly she was glad of it.

"Cheers," Mark said, and touched the rim of his glass to hers.

She drank because not to would have been even more uncomfortable. The bubbles fizzed on her tongue and she swallowed, wondering if the alcohol would help her relax.

"I haven't seen you since..." He frowned. "Since the charity event in London."

"Three years," she said, pasting on the smile that she'd worn all damn day.

"Amazing how we keep missing each other, in all that time."

It wasn't amazing at all. Charlotte generally stayed on her side of the Atlantic. And rekindling anything with Mark wasn't on her agenda.

"Isn't it?"

"You're looking gorgeous. Even more beautiful than you were then. I take it that's an Aurora design?"

"Of course." She cradled the champagne glass. "I wouldn't wear anything else."

"It's very timeless. I mean, your mother would look smashing in it."

And there it was. The subtle little dig, the slight criticism that had always turned her off. "I'll be sure to tell her you said so. Now if you'll excuse me…"

She went to move away but he reached out and grabbed her wrist. They were close enough now she could smell the booze and knew he'd been drinking for a while, though he hid it well. A wave of revulsion rolled through her. She hadn't forgotten that Mark Church was the kind of man who would say whatever he needed to get what he wanted.

"Let's get out of here and go someplace quieter," he suggested, his dark eyes meeting hers. "For old times' sake."

She pulled her wrist away just as she became aware of Jacob coming forward. "What a kind suggestion, but no thank you."

He slid closer. "Come on, Charlotte. We were good together. Let's see how it—"

"Ah, there you are." Jacob's voice was measured and calm. "I wondered if you'd been held up." His eyes smiled down into hers, and then she watched as he turned his icy gaze on Mark. "And you are?"

Mark, being the idiot he was, straightened his shoulders and lifted his chin, which still left him a few inches shorter than Jacob. "Mark Church." He didn't ask Jacob his name, which seemed totally in character.

"Nice to meet you. Charlotte, darling..." Charlotte nearly rolled her eyes at his deliberate overplay of "darling" in a very posh Londony type of accent. "Shall we get back?"

"Of course." She was so grateful for the save.

They'd just started to move away when Mark stepped forward again. "Charlotte, remember what I said. We're both in town all week."

Gross. As if she'd hook up with him again after all this time. But she didn't have to worry. Jacob let go of her hand and stepped up to Mark, face-to-face, and Charlotte wanted to laugh at the sheer difference in their physiques. Mark's expression turned to one of childish defiance.

"Not cool, Mark. I'm standing right here. And I recall the lady saying no. That's all it takes, right? No?"

"Sure, mate." Mark replied in a fake accent that made him seem even more ridiculous.

Charlotte took Jacob's hand again, so very grateful he was with her despite her protests that she didn't need a bodyguard.

And when Mark muttered a word that equated Jacob to a particular piece of anatomy, Charlotte wasn't so sure Jacob wouldn't turn around.

Instead Jacob laughed and shook his head. "All booze and no brains," he muttered. "And not worth it. Unless you want me to."

"I don't want a scene," she said back. "But thank you, Jacob. I don't think I need a bodyguard, but I'm awfully glad you were my wingman tonight."

He stopped and faced her, and there was something different in his expression. Something softer and more personal.

"I know you said you were supposed to stay for a few hours, but you're exhausted. Why don't we go?"

A headache was starting to brew behind her eyes. "Let's try another half hour. We'll go in, make another circuit around and then, yes, we can go. I didn't expect the time difference to affect me quite this much."

"As long as we keep you away from what's-his-name." Jacob smiled, and her heart did another one of those irregular beats. He didn't smile often, but when he did, it was like a bright ray of sunshine.

"He's an ex for a reason," she replied, raising her voice as they entered the room once again. "I'm truly not interested."

Another glass of champagne was pressed into her hand—that made three now, and nowhere near her normal limit but more than enough on her empty stomach. Jacob stayed close beside her, engaging in brief conversation when invited. She got the feeling he knew how to be quite the chameleon. For all he was a former soldier, he knew how to clean up and be very charming.

They were making their way to the door now and Charlotte was feeling the effects of the champagne. Her legs were a little wobbly, and she felt like her smile was maybe a bit too wide. She looked over at Jacob. He was still calm and cool, looking so suave in his suit and with his hair slicked back. Like a dressed-up Nordic warrior or something.

"What?" he asked, when he noticed her staring at him.

"Nothing. You're just…never mind."

"Fine. Let's get out of here, shall we? You've done your duty rounds."

They headed to the door only to be faced with Mark again, his back to the bar, staring at them.

Charlotte's head began to throb in time with the music. Then she felt Jacob's arm around her waist, pulling her close to his side.

"One minute and we're home free," his voice rumbled in her ear, and she shivered.

He guided her out of the room and to the quiet area where the coat check was. "Come on, let's get you something to eat. You need to sop up that champagne."

"Where?"

He laughed. "This is New York. Finding you a hamburger won't be difficult."

Oh, a hamburger sounded scrumptious. And maybe french fries, and lots of ketchup.

Jacob called for their car and they waited in the lobby for it to arrive. By this point, Charlotte was really regretting the champagne and not more water, and also not eating something for dinner before arriving. Her head was light and with a strange pounding, and she was sure she could hear her stomach growling over the other sounds in the hotel lobby.

"He's here," Jacob said, and took her arm and led her out to the waiting car.

He tucked her inside, then asked the driver to find a good burger joint not far from the apartment. It wasn't too long and they'd pulled up in front of a Shake Shack.

"I'm going in there...in this?"

"Why not?"

She studied him for a moment, then thought to herself, *Why not?* It was probably the most spontaneous thing Jacob would agree to all week. She giggled a little thinking about it. "Do you need to go inside and make sure it's safe first?"

He raised an eyebrow. "Great. A few glasses of fizz and you're a laugh a minute."

"Why, thank you."

He asked the driver to wait, and then they went in. It was ten thirty, still early, and there was a scattering of people inside. As far as she could tell, she was the only one in a designer dress and four-inch heels.

"Cheeseburger?" he asked her.

"God, yes. That sounds perfect."

He stepped up and ordered two cheeseburgers, fries and, after consulting with her, lemonade. They sat at one of the tables, and Charlotte started to laugh.

"What?"

"This is so strange. But fun! Thank you." She reached for a fry and dipped it in ketchup. "Oh, my God. This is so good."

He unwrapped his burger. "Eat something. I've never seen someone get so wobbly on a few ounces of champagne."

"That's unusual for me, but I'm tired. And I didn't eat enough."

"I know." He wiped his lips with his napkin and took a sip of lemonade. "I checked the agenda for tomorrow. You're heading to a show at ten."

"I'll take in some shows and then I have a conference call with the Paris office at two."

"That's late for Paris. The workday will be winding up."

"We adjusted it to suit my itinerary," she admitted. "Tomorrow night I have a dinner and another party." She took a bite of the cheeseburger and nearly moaned in appreciation. "Who knew a fast-food burger would taste so good?"

She was careful not to drip, and leaned over the tray so nothing dropped on her cashmere coat or onto her dress. It was no time at all and the burger was gone. She looked up and found Jacob laughing at her.

"Okay, so that wasn't very dignified. I was starving." She reached out for another fry and popped it in her mouth.

"It's great. You know, you are defying all my expectations of you."

"You had expectations?"

"Sure. At first, I figured you would be a spoiled rich girl, coming to New York to party for a week. Which you are, but I've discovered you're not a party girl. Not like some of the people back there." He shook his head.

"Oh, so judgy," she replied, sipping the tart lemonade. "There's nothing wrong with working hard and playing hard, and everyone in that room knows how to work hard."

"Point taken," he said, pointing a fry at her. "But you...you get a look in your eye. You're driven by something."

Wow. That hit a little close to home. She took a long drink of lemonade and avoided his probing. "Aren't we all?" she said instead.

His gray gaze held hers. "Yes, I think we are."

She wondered what drove him. Transitioning from soldier to security was a logical step, but why? Or more precisely, why now? He was maybe mid, late thirties. He said he'd been wounded, but clearly that was not an issue now. So why had he quit?

But then...none of her business. And she suspected if she'd ask, that was the answer she'd get, too.

She grabbed two more french fries, but he reached at the same time and their fingers touched.

He pulled his back quickly and a sliver of something zinged through her stomach. She looked up but he was busy crumpling up his napkin and tidying up. Interesting. A little jolt of attraction, and not just on her part. He'd reacted as if her fingers had burned him.

"So that guy back there, Mark. I take it you guys were a thing at one time."

"We were, regretfully. I think every woman, at some point in their dating lives, meets one guy who breaks their heart and steals their innocence about the fairy tale of true and perfect love. That was Mark for me."

He sat back, eyebrows raised in surprise. "He did all that, and you were just…so poised."

"He got the better of me once. He won't again."

"What happened?"

"He wanted my connections more than he wanted me. He also wanted connections with some other major players. None of us knew about the others. Until… Well, I guess I was the last one to figure it out. I was only twenty-two."

Jacob made a sound of disgust in his throat.

"Exactly. I overheard gossip about him sleeping with all three of us. I honestly thought I was going to be sick. When I confronted him about it, he said that this was how the game was played."

"And you said?"

"I said I wasn't into games, and that we were over. I'm sure I seemed very strong and decisive. Inside I was a wreck. I've managed to avoid him ever since. Until tonight."

"And he propositioned you?"

"He's greasier than that burger I just ate."

Jacob laughed then, a rich, warm sound that reached in and thawed all the frozen places inside. Second surprise of the night: Jacob Wolfe was actually quite likable when he was being human.

"Anyway, enough of my sordid romantic past. I'm full," she announced, and wiped her fingers. "Shall we go?"

"Of course," he answered, and sent her a genuine, warm smile. Oh, she was going to have to watch out for that.

The ride to the apartment was short, and it seemed they barely got in the car and then they were at the tall gray building. The park loomed to the left, across the street, tree branches bare and snow still covering the grass. She loved Central Park, but right now it looked cold and uninviting.

Unlike the Aurora Inc. apartment. It was warm and bathed in mellow light from lit lamps. The housekeeper had been in during the day and made everything shipshape. Charlotte let out a sigh of relief and wilted a little, unbuttoning her coat.

To her surprise, Jacob slid the coat off her shoulders and took it to the hidden closet where he carefully hung it up. When he turned back, she was watching him, as an awareness settled in the air.

Oh, my.

"Do you always wear black and white?" he asked suddenly.

She looked down at her dress, and then back up. "Well, a lot. It's the Aurora signature colors."

"So it's a statement?"

"Yes. It's…on brand."

He frowned a little.

"What?"

"It's just…never mind. It's none of my business and you're clearly the one in fashion."

Now she was intrigued, because to her great surprise, twin dots of color showed on his cheeks. "What, Jacob? What were you going to say?"

He cleared his throat. "You're a beautiful woman. Why wouldn't you want to stand out? In bold colors, like the birds I used to see in South America. Dramatic plumage that would take my breath away."

Her heart started tapping out a strange rhythm. "I'm not sure it's wise for me to take your breath away," she murmured.

His gaze held hers. "Too late."

"Jacob…"

He cleared his throat again. "That's all I'm

going to say about that, and it was probably too much."

He turned to leave the foyer but she stopped him. "Thank you, for what you did tonight. With Mark."

"It's my job." She wondered if he was reminding her or himself. Because when he'd gone back and said "not cool," it hadn't felt like someone doing just a job.

"You could have been more...bodyguardish. But it felt like having a friend in my corner. So even if you're on the payroll, I appreciate how you handled this evening." She smiled. "Including the cheeseburger, which I needed very much, and the ear. I feel a lot better."

"Good. Get some rest, Charlotte. Your week is just getting started."

He moved beside her for a moment, and she caught the scent of his aftershave as he passed by and checked to ensure the door was locked.

Because it was his job. She couldn't forget that. Even if she was now feeling as if she'd overshared.

"Good night, Jacob."

"Good night."

Then he disappeared down the hallway to his room, and she heard the soft click of the bedroom door as he shut it.

She hadn't imagined it, right? There'd been

something. When their fingers had touched and just now, when he'd looked at her. And admitted she took his breath away.

This trip might end up being more interesting than she planned. And that was saying something...

CHAPTER FIVE

JACOB WAS A damned idiot.

He'd crossed a line last night. First, when his gut had burned when he'd seen that slime ball Mark trying to make nice. Then when they'd gone to the burger joint. A simple touch of fingers shouldn't have caused such a reaction, and he'd pulled away like he was fourteen years old.

But worst of all was what he'd said when they'd arrived home. That she'd taken his breath away? He looked up at the ceiling and scowled. He didn't do romantic gestures. He didn't get emotionally involved...ever. Not since Jacinta.

His stomach knotted as the familiar weight of self-loathing settled over him. He had known that the mission always, always came first. And instead he'd let himself get wrapped up in her. An asset to their mission with wide, dark eyes and soft lips. She'd made him laugh despite the danger. Made him think and do a lot of things. And that had gotten her killed.

He should have let it go by now; it was years ago. But he couldn't, because the consequences had been too severe and he'd stopped trusting himself. It had prompted his retirement more than any gunshot wound.

He threw off the covers and swung his legs over the edge of the bed. Five a.m. The gym in the building was state of the art, and yesterday there'd been one other person in there with him. Nice and quiet, just the way he liked it, so he could hear his heart beat in his ears and the clank of weight plates.

He set his jaw and went to wake Charlotte. Last night he'd forgotten his promise to be tough on her after yesterday morning, but today he was reminded. He'd told her he would drag her to the gym because he couldn't trust her to follow instructions. Maybe they both needed to be reminded of that.

He put on shorts and a T-shirt and then went next door and knocked on her door. Loudly.

Time to get back on the job and stop being foolish.

Charlotte pulled the pillow over her head. What was that awful noise? Persistent thumping was coming from somewhere… She pulled the pillow off again and realized it was her bedroom door.

"What?" she yelled, irritated. She hated being awakened.

"Rise and shine, buttercup. Time for the gym."

Oh, no. No, he wouldn't. Sure, she'd gone out yesterday when she'd promised she wouldn't, but the day had ended so nicely. Nicely enough she'd lain awake for an hour after going to bed, just thinking about it. "I'm sleeping!"

"No, you're not or you wouldn't be yelling at me. I told you I wouldn't give up my workouts, so up and at 'em, sunshine. Pull on some spandex and let's go."

She growled and rolled over, pulling the covers over her head. It wasn't enough to block out his voice, though. "If you're not up in ten seconds, I'm coming in. Ten…nine—"

"Fine, I'm up!" she snapped, throwing off the covers. She went to the door and flung it open. "I'm up. Now please go away."

Jacob had been ready to say "eight" and his mouth now hung open and his eyes widened. She realized belatedly that she was wearing a short silk nightie that covered everything important but didn't leave a whole lot to the imagination. She stepped back and slammed the door in his face as heat rushed up into her cheeks.

She would have to act as if nothing had happened. And he wasn't going to leave her alone, so she went to her drawers and pulled out a pair of yoga pants and a fitted top that she normally wore for her irregular yoga practice. She always traveled with it just in case she ended up stressed out and in need of some stretching and deep breathing. And boy, could she use that today.

Only there'd be no Zen, would there? Because they were going to the gym. Ugh.

She wrenched the door open again to find him still standing there, the stunned look gone from his face. Thank God. "Fine," she said, her voice sharp with annoyance. "If I must, I must. Though I might want to remind you that you work for me."

"Oh, la dee da, there's the princess." His eyes lit with humor that only infuriated her more. "Technically, I work for your mother, so that actually puts me in charge. Let's go. Bring music if you want. As long as I can see you, that's fine. No need to chat."

She grabbed her mobile and a pair of wireless earbuds, thinking that the moment from last night had to be an utter blip, because she was back to despising him again. She said nothing to him in the elevator, and when they entered the gym, he went his way and she went to the other side and the cardio machines.

She hated running and wasn't a fan of stationary bikes, so she chose an elliptical and put it on the easiest setting. Playlist blaring in her ears, she hit the start button and started the smooth yet slightly awkward motion of the machine.

Five minutes later she was thinking how out of shape she was. Granted, she led a busy life and walked a lot and tried to eat well so she kept her trim figure. And the genetics from her mother's side didn't hurt, either. But as far as cardio health… Her breath was labored and she knew her face was turning red from the exertion. Worse, this was how Jacob was going to see her.

It made her feel naked. She worked very hard to not show anyone her weaknesses or insecurities. She was Charlotte Pemberton. There was an image to uphold.

She stole a glance over at Jacob and tried not to goggle. He was lying flat on a bench doing chest presses, and his whole upper body flexed as the bar and plates went up and down, up and down, at least ten times. He was…beautiful, she realized. In a rugged, angular, rough sort of way. Her body clenched as she watched him put the bar back in the bracket, and then she looked away before he could catch her staring.

The next time she glanced over, he'd removed his T-shirt and was wiping his face with it. He had abs. Like six-pack abs that glistened with sweat. He dropped the shirt and went to a ma-

chine that had two handles sticking out. He
braced his elbows, held onto the handles and
lifted his knees in an ab crunch that made those
ridges bunch and flex.

Good heavens. She lost her rhythm on the elliptical and had to regain it. She supposed this
was the equivalent of her opening the door in
her negligee this morning. At least maybe he'd
liked what he'd seen?

Though why should it matter?

After torturing herself for thirty minutes, she
finally stopped the machine and went to the
water cooler for a drink. She'd turned off her
playlist just in case he said something, but he
was now over at the leg press. It didn't seem
possible that he could push that much weight
with his legs, but the black plates moved back
and forth in a steady rhythm.

The man was in stellar shape.

Charlotte was much too embarrassed to at-
tempt to do any weights with him around, considering how puny her muscles were, so she
went to a treadmill instead and started to walk.
It was easier, she supposed, if not a bit monot-
onous. If he were going to make her go to the
gym, fine. What she did when she got here was
none of his business. If she wanted to walk,
dammit, she'd walk.

But as she watched him move to adjust his

weights, she hit a button and added an incline. Just because.

He kept her there for a whole hour. When he finished, he put his sweat-streaked T-shirt back over his head and came over to the treadmill.

"You set?"

She scowled. To be honest, she felt pretty good, now that she'd gotten moving, but she wouldn't say as much to him. "I'm ready."

They went back up in the elevator without saying a word. Once they got back to the apartment, he opened the door and let her in first, then followed and locked it again. "I'm going to shower. What time do we need to leave?"

She looked at her phone. It wasn't even six thirty yet. Normally she would sleep for another hour. "Nine. Different venue today. But I'm sure you know that. It must be on your itinerary."

"Of course. Make sure you eat something before we go. I don't want you fainting away today."

"Yes, master," she said darkly. He was really enjoying bossing her around, wasn't he?

But when she got under the hot spray of the shower all she could think about was him, and his crazy-hard body, and how he'd lost his speech when she'd opened the door to her bedroom this morning. She had the reckless and insane thought that she'd love to walk into *his* room right now, and step into his shower, with all the steam and soap and skin.

Oh, for Pete's sake. She was fantasizing about her bodyguard now, and how dumb was that? It was Sunday; on Saturday they'd be packing up and heading back to Heathrow. She would never see him again. Last night they'd got a little too personal, but it didn't have to happen again.

She dried off and went to search her spreadsheet for today's wardrobe choice. As she was finding the app she used, she realized how very boring and predictable that sounded. She'd planned her wardrobe two weeks ago. Whatever happened to wearing what you felt like?

The app popped up with today's choices: matching bra and panty set, dress, shoes, accessories. The dress was white with a vertical black stripe straight down the middle, ending just above the knee, blending class and sex appeal with the fitted shape. Black stilettos rounded out the ensemble, but as she looked at the items laid out on her bed, she thought back to last night and Jacob's comment that the black and white was somehow boring.

It was on brand. It said *Aurora*… But it didn't say *Charlotte*.

She dressed, but the whole time her mind was working. She'd spent years trying to never cause ripples. She'd fallen in love with the wrong kind of person and had broken it off to save the family—and herself—the embarrassment. She never, ever created waves. But in all that... The woman she'd become was buried underneath the company image. Until recently, it hadn't felt constricting. But it did now.

By the time she'd finished her hair and makeup, she was ready for some breakfast and she'd come up with a plan to shake things up a little.

And if it knocked Jacob's eyeballs out of his head, so much the better. That would teach him for dragging her to the gym before 6:00 a.m.!

Jacob was still in awe of Charlotte's work ethic. She put on her "work" face the moment she entered the public and it never faltered. Even when she was seated and watching, he could tell her mind was turning. She stared so intently and never moved, almost as if cataloging things in her head. Every time they got in the car she wilted a little, had a bottle of water and, if time, a snack. He didn't try to make conversation. He simply let her recharge in the silence.

He wondered if she knew how intimidating she was. And not in a scary, bad way, but in a "she's so capable and put together" way. It was as if she was determined no one ever see a weakness or chink in her armor. Even last night, with Mark, she'd been remarkably composed.

He'd been surprised that she'd shared something so personal with him. And it made her seem less of a client and more of...

Nope. He couldn't let his mind go there. It was bad enough he kept seeing her in that tiny nightie, her eyes flashing. Thank God she'd slammed the door in his face. And then watching her trim figure on the elliptical... He'd punished himself with the weights to keep himself distracted.

She had a conference call later in the afternoon, so he was surprised when they got into the car after yet another show that had bored him to tears, and she asked the driver to take her to the Aurora store on Fifth Avenue.

"This isn't on your itinerary."

"No, it's not. I want to pick up a few things. Besides, it makes sense for me to stop into the New York store. The general manager is a new hire, just last year."

"Fine... But I'm going in with you."

In fact, it was bothering him that things had been so quiet. Other than the incident at the party last night, there hadn't been a peep from whoever had been sending the threatening emails. He wondered if that meant the perpetrator was based in Paris or London, which was highly likely. But a pattern of emails every few weeks and then nothing didn't sit well with him. It was waiting for the other shoe to drop.

The Aurora store was unbelievably elegant. Everything was white, black, or chrome, and the employees dressed all in black. Charlotte looked around and Jacob looked at her. She couldn't have had more than five hours of sleep last night and she was fresh and energetic, or at least doing a reasonable impression of it. She gave an associate a genuine smile as she approached, and said, "Hello, I'm Charlotte Pemberton."

"Of course. Good afternoon, Ms. Pemberton. What a pleasure to have you in the store today."

He'd give the associate credit; she maintained impeccable composure when faced with one of the Pemberton family.

"I'm actually here to do some shopping and say hello to Ms. Walker-Barnes."

"Let me call up to let her assistant know you're here, and then I can assist you, if you like."

"That would be lovely, thank you…" She looked at the silver-plated name tag. "Donatella." She laughed. "What a great name for working in fashion."

They shared a smile, and then Donatella excused herself briefly.

"You're shopping?" Jacob asked, surprised.

"I am. You would undoubtedly find it boring, but I'm sure we can find you a spot to sit and wait with a good vantage point for picking out any danger."

She was being a bit of a brat, and he kind of liked it. He liked when she was sassy.

It didn't take long for word to spread that one of the Pemberton family was in house. Jacob watched the buzz around him as Charlotte and Donatella disappeared into the racks of clothing. From his vantage point, he could see the door and anyone who entered, as well as keep a good eye on the traffic within the store, patron and employee alike. Charlotte disappeared into the changing area and Donatella zipped back and forth with clothing items for Charlotte to try on.

He tried not to picture it, but it was hard. Since she'd opened the door this morning in a barely there nightie, he'd had trouble erasing the picture from his mind. Her clothing style looked wonderful, but it hid the lovely length of her legs and the fullness of her breasts.

It was over an hour later when Charlotte emerged, her face triumphant, carrying two large bags in her hands.

"Ready?" He wasn't sure what put the pleased flush on her cheeks, but she looked gorgeous. More animated than he could remember.

"I'm going upstairs to meet with the GM briefly. You can follow along if you like. Or stay down here. Your choice."

He'd had a chance to look over much of the offerings on the main floor, which consisted of the fashion department. The whole thing was impressive and intimidating. Despite his expensive suit, he felt remarkably out of place. But he was curious. What did the upper floor hold?

"I'll come with you. I don't think I need to follow you into the office, though." He smiled at her. "Do you want me to carry your bags?"

She shook her head. "That's not your job, Jacob. Besides, they're not heavy."

He appreciated that. A princess would have wanted someone to carry her bags and be, well, subservient, he thought. Hardly ever did she pull any diva behavior.

The second floor was full of gorgeous lighting and glass cases, all showcasing Aurora's cosmetics, scent, and jewelry offerings. The makeup didn't interest him at all, but as Charlotte disappeared down a hallway to the offices, Jacob perused the jewelry cases.

"May I help you find something, sir?"

He looked up to find a lovely woman smiling at him expectantly. He wanted to say yes. He could afford it, after all, a fact not many people realized. Wolfe Security had proved to be very lucrative in the three years he'd been running it, and his needs were simple. No, the thing preventing him from buying any jewelry at all was that he didn't have anyone to buy it *for*.

He thought of Charlotte and realized how ridiculous it would be for him to buy her anything. And yet… He couldn't deny he had the urge to. He found himself saying, "Maybe something, I don't know, unusual. Distinct."

"Are you looking for a ring? Necklace, maybe a bracelet?"

He floundered. "I don't know."

"Well, what's she like? What does she normally wear for jewelry?"

He thought for a moment about the last three days. He'd seen her with pearls, maybe, but truly he hadn't noticed anything major, so his guess was that she went for an understated look.

"She doesn't wear anything big, I don't think," he answered tentatively. "It's like she tries not to stand out. But she stands out anyway. I wish she knew how beautiful she is."

Oh, no. Had that just come out of his mouth? It was true, after all, but what surprised him was that he'd *noticed*.

"She sounds absolutely lovely."

He didn't know what else to say, so he followed as she led the way past the case in front of them to another section. "We've got some lovely pieces here, a little less traditional, a little more colorful. Things that stand out, but maybe not too much? How about this?"

She reached into the display and removed one of the most beautiful pieces of jewelry he'd ever seen. It wasn't just a necklace, it was art. A butterfly, suspended by a platinum chain, with a rainbow of colors sparkling in the gems within. "That's stunning," he admitted.

"The setting and chain are both platinum, and the gemstones include aquamarine, peridot, pink sapphire and, of course, diamonds." She turned it over in her hand. "It's bold without being brash, beautiful and yet not flashy or ostentatious."

He took it into his palm, feeling the weight of it. Nothing flimsy or fragile; the piece had weight to it, a stability that he liked. And the butterfly… It would suit her. She was far more gorgeous than she let on, but like the butterfly, she wasn't brash or flashy.

He shouldn't buy it. He could never give it to her. A part of him was terrified that he wanted to. Another part was amazed, because he never thought he'd want to feel this way ever again.

Alive.

"Wrap it up," he said, before he could think twice.

"Yes, sir." She smiled at him and he waited

while she went through the process of boxing it, putting it in the distinctive Aurora bag and running his credit card.

He tucked the little bag into his coat pocket, where the weight of it reminded him of how foolish he was being. Why buy something that would simply sit in his house, tucked away in a drawer somewhere? He didn't want to think about it too much. It had been an impulse and that was the end of it.

And then Charlotte came out of the office and down the hall, talking and laughing with another woman, and his body reacted before he had a chance to tamp down any response. Her lips were curved in a wide smile and her hair swung across her face a little. She had her coat on and her shopping bags were clutched in her hands.

When she saw him, her smile stayed in place and she made introductions. "Janet, this is Jacob Wolfe. Jacob, the New York general manager, Janet Walker-Barnes."

"It's a pleasure," Janet said, holding out her hand, which he shook.

"Likewise," he replied, and glanced over at Charlotte. Any other time she'd introduced him only as Jacob. Today she'd used his surname. Which meant all Janet Walker-Barnes had to do was go to Google and she'd know who he was.

Charlotte must trust her, then. And that intrigued him.

"It was so good to see you, Janet." Charlotte leaned forward and bussed Janet's cheek. "And I'll see you in a few months at the GM summit, yes?"

"Of course. I wouldn't miss Paris for the world."

Charlotte beamed up at him. "I'm ready now. Thank you for waiting for me."

"Of course." He looked down at her and felt that confusion bubble in his chest again. "It was nice to meet you," he said to Janet.

"You, as well." She smiled widely, and then turned a knowing glance to Charlotte. "I'll see you on Wednesday?"

"Of course. And what we discussed… That won't be an issue?"

"I'll handle everything, and check in with the team."

"You're a gem."

They said their goodbyes and made their way to the escalator. "What was that about?" Jacob asked.

"Oh, work stuff," she said lightly, and he got the sense there was more to the answer she wasn't sharing.

"And you used my full name. You like this woman a lot, don't you?"

"I do. I met her just before she took on the position. We flew her to Paris for her final interview and she and I really hit it off. She's young enough to be so full of energy and fun but old enough to have significant experience. She was an assistant manager at one of our biggest competitors, and a real find."

He guessed Janet to be late thirties, maybe forty. For some reason, Charlotte's description niggled. Janet was more…his age. Did she assess him in the same way? With "significant experience"?

They headed back to the apartment, and Jacob said no more about it. And then, once inside, he went to his room, took the small bag out of his pocket and tucked it in the dresser, under his socks.

CHAPTER SIX

WHEN CHARLOTTE STEPPED out of her bedroom the next morning, she pressed a hand to her belly and let out a slow breath. It was just Jacob, after all, but he was the one who had brought up the black and white and her appearance. Yesterday's trip to the Aurora store had been a success, and today she was trying out the first of her purchases—a turquoise dress in her usual style but the color so vivid that she felt utterly conspicuous.

She was a confident woman who was dedicated to the family company. But after Jacob's comments the other night, she wondered if she'd sacrificed her own identity for it more than she realized. Aurora was the family business and where she worked... But it wasn't who she was. Or maybe it was, and that unsettled her. Surely she was more than the company.

Maybe if she really wanted to stand on her own at Aurora, she first needed to stand out.

Jacob was in the kitchen, and she could smell eggs cooking and the yeasty scent of bread in the toaster. He'd made her go to the gym again this morning but she hadn't minded as much. Last night they'd gotten in around ten. She'd gone to the dinner party and then another event where she put in a brief appearance and left. Charlotte had never been one to party into the wee hours and run on three hours sleep and an energy drink.

"Good morning," she said, stepping to the threshold.

He turned around and his eyes widened, then a grin blossomed on his face. "Well. Not a bit of black in sight. You look great."

She let out the breath she was holding and smiled back. "My shopping trip yesterday. What you said the other night got me thinking. I like bright colors. And the Aurora color theme is black and white, but that's not our entire brand. A brand is so much more than a color scheme. So why not change my wardrobe up a little?"

He scooped eggs onto two plates, plopped a piece of toast on each, and gestured to the barstools and counter. "Breakfast is ready."

"You didn't have to do that for me."

"I was making it for me anyway. What's another egg and slice of bread?"

It was almost a little too domestic, but truthfully when the family was in residence they had a housekeeper come in only a few times a week. They mostly cooked and tidied for themselves. It gave them more privacy. This week, she was barely at the apartment anyway. There was no need for them to have a cook and in-house staff.

"Well, I appreciate it anyway since I know it's not in your job description."

He spread an obscene amount of jelly on his toast. "So seriously, you always wear black and white?"

She met his gaze as she speared a piece of egg with her fork. "Not always, but when I'm on Aurora business, yes."

"But why?"

She thought about it as she ate, and then got up and went to the fridge to get the orange juice. "To be honest," she answered, turning the cap on the juice, "I think it has been a need to do everything right. To…" She hesitated as a lightbulb seemed to flick on in her mind. "Well, without giving you the fine details, Stephen is the earl and the heir. Bella did something foolish when she was younger that caused my parents a great deal of worry. William, my twin, was a real wild child for a while, and my parents also practically raised my cousin, Christophe, who came with a bit of family drama. So me? I tried to stay under the radar, no extra trouble." Even if that came at a personal cost.

"I see." He tapped his chin. "And yet, for someone who wants to be under the radar, you lead the public relations department. You are the face of Aurora in that way."

"Only as the spokesperson. The idea is for me to focus the light on the company, not me personally."

"The light's going to be on you today," he said, nodding at her. "That, Ms. Pemberton, is a serious plumage color."

She tucked her hair behind her ear as she looked down at her plate, a little embarrassed. Still, she loved the shade of blue and she'd paired it with a favorite pair of neutral heels and her special diamond earrings.

And yet later, when she stepped out of the car and into the venue, she felt just a tiny bit empowered. It was odd how a few yards of bright fabric stitched together could make such a difference. For once, she wasn't merely an extension of the company. She was her own woman. It seemed unbelievable that it was because a man she barely knew had a keen insight into her behavior.

She changed out of the dress later that afternoon, upon arriving back at the apartment. Jacob was in his room and she'd put on casual trousers and a sweater to think about dinner. Charlotte had had a great day, but the prospect of cooking a dinner only to go out again later seemed too daunting. Tonight's party was a big deal, a celebrity-studded event at some converted warehouse in Brooklyn. If Jacob had been surprised at the guest list at the previous events, tonight he'd be overwhelmed. She was kind of looking forward to it, actually.

But not making dinner. So she grabbed her phone, found a bookmarked pizza place and put in an order. She'd go easy now, because she had a killer dress to fit into. And then when they got home, cold pizza would be the perfect snack.

She'd just placed the order when her phone rang, and she could see it was her mother. She hurried to hit the little green symbol on the screen. "Maman! Bonjour!"

"Bonjour, *ma petite*!" Aurora's charming voice came over the phone. "I saw photos of you already today… I absolutely loved your dress."

"Really? It's not…me."

"Oh, I think it is. You're a beautiful bird, Charlotte, but you hide behind things. I was thrilled to see your colorful feathers today."

"Why didn't you say anything before? I was trying to fit with Aurora's image, you know."

Her mother's rusty laugh came through the phone. "My darling, this company was not built by someone trying to fit in or hide. I brought the brazen attitude, and your father brought the class and elegance. You've got that same spirit, you know. Especially when it comes to the company. It's time you stepped into your role here with your own personality. Today was a baby step, yes?"

She blinked back tears, realizing how relieved she was at the praise and support. "Yes, Maman, it was. I went to the store yesterday and bought straight off the rack."

Again the rusty laugh came over the line. "Of course you did, and bravo. How are things otherwise? We didn't get a chance to catch up on yesterday's conference call."

They chatted for a while until the doorman called up. "I'm sorry, Maman, I need to go. I ordered pizza for dinner. I couldn't bear to make even a sandwich tonight with another party on the diary."

"You're feeding Mr. Wolfe as well, I assume."

"Yes. I still don't know why I need him, but he's not so bad." She hoped her voice didn't betray her. She did far too much fantasizing about him and put too much weight in his opinion. It didn't help that her mother had used the same comparison as he had—that she was a colorful bird.

"You go eat and check in with me soon. I'm

missing New York, but you're doing a fabulous job."

"*Je t'aime*, Maman," Charlotte said. "I'll call you soon." Then when she hung up, she called down the hall. "Jacob? I'm going to grab the pizza I ordered, okay?"

His door opened immediately, and he came out, still dressed in his suit trousers, shirt and tie. "I can go. I heard you on the phone and didn't want to interrupt."

When he returned, they sat at the kitchen counter yet again and ate. The pizza was perfect: the crust not too thick and not too thin, with a crispy bottom, spicy sauce, savory sausage, mushrooms, and just the right amount of mozzarella. Charlotte went to the fridge and got a big bottle of Perrier and poured them each a glass.

"I wish I didn't have to go out tonight," she admitted.

"You could always skip it," he mused, taking another slice of pizza.

"Are you kidding? This is a huge deal. I just need to gear myself up. I've got a killer dress, too." She grinned. "A little more risqué than I usually wear."

Did he reach for his water a little too quickly? It was nice to think that she might be able to cause that kind of reaction in him when he was usually so placid and unshakeable.

"And will there be any exes to fend off?" He raised an eyebrow. "Just to be prepared."

"Don't worry. I doubt Mark will have an invitation to this one. And maybe it will surprise you to know that there aren't many exes in my past."

He hesitated and then said, "I'm sorry. I shouldn't have been like that."

"You were teasing. But maybe I wanted you to know anyway."

That heavy, wonderful feeling settled around them again, that simple knowledge that they were two people who found each other attractive, but shouldn't.

"Charlotte…"

She felt daring. "Mmm. I like it when you say my name like that."

"Charlotte!" Harsher this time.

"Jacob!" she mocked.

He pushed back from the counter, the stool legs scraping against the floor. "Don't." His mouth set in a firm line. "Don't flirt with me."

There was something behind his eyes just then that made her cease. It wasn't his words, but something more. A flicker of anger, of pain perhaps. It occurred to her that she didn't know him at all beyond the fact that he was former military and now a bodyguard. Did he have a family? Was he in love with someone? Where did he live? She knew none of those things. It surprised her that she wanted to.

"I'm sorry," she murmured. "I *was* flirting. But not trying to play with you. There's a difference. It won't happen again."

She'd swiveled on the stool and faced him. Now his gaze delved into hers and for a breathless moment she thought he was going to kiss her. He stared at her lips for a prolonged second and then back up into her eyes, and she saw regret mixed with the other emotions on his face.

"I can't. I won't. You understand that, right?"

She nodded quickly. The way he said it, everything about this moment, told her he wanted to. How quickly it had escalated from a tiny bit of teasing to desire.

She desired him. There was no denying it, not to herself.

"I understand," she whispered. "I never considered that there might be someone else. I don't even know much about you. It was inconsiderate of me."

"There's no one else," he said harshly. "No one."

He turned and walked away, leaving her there with a half-full pizza box and the dirty dishes. And she didn't mind a bit. Because today she'd felt more alive than she'd felt in years, and it was all because of Jacob Wolfe. The way he'd said there was no one else, so sharp and edged with pain? That told her that there had been, once. And she suspected that his heartbreak might have been more devastating than hers.

She cleaned up the mess and decided to do a quick email check before dressing for the party. It was no time at all and her laptop was booting up on the countertop. She hummed a little as she logged in and then clicked on the email icon. Her inbox popped up and she waited for messages to download.

There were twelve, and one stood out and made her heart stop.

Fingers shaking, she used the trackpad to scroll to the line in her inbox and tapped to open it.

HOW DARE YOU? BITCH.

She right-clicked on a tiny icon to download the picture, and then stepped back from the computer in shock.

There'd never been a picture before. And this one was so very personal.

"Jacob?" Her throat closed over and she called out again, the sound strangled. "Jacob?"

Jacob heard her calling from his room, and something in her voice put him on alert. He'd been sitting on the end of his bed, trying to sort through his thoughts and emotions after what just had—and hadn't—happened in the kitchen. But her tone... Something was wrong. He got up and immediately went to her.

She was standing four feet away from her laptop, but even before he got to her he could see what was on her screen. A photo from today, her beautiful blue dress, and slash marks cut across it. And one right across her face.

He saw the words, too, as he moved closer. "'How dare you?' How dare you what?" He turned around to face her. The color had leached out of her face and she was shaking. "This is definitely an escalation from the other letters."

"You think?" Her voice shook, but he sensed it was a small part fear and another part anger. "How dare I what? This is crazy."

"But to add the slash marks... Whoever is sending the messages is furious with you, Charlotte. And this is the first time violence has been implied."

"I know. *I know.*" She stood back and clenched her fists. "The original photo is on the internet, so it doesn't mean whoever is behind it is here in New York."

"It doesn't mean they aren't, either," he reasoned. "But more than that for now, are you okay?"

She turned to him, her eyes blazing. "Oh, I'm fine. Now I'm not just annoyed, I'm angry."

He chuckled a little, admiring her feistiness. "Just don't let your anger make you foolish."

"I won't."

"I need to send this off to your IT people."

Her gaze snapped to his. "I'd rather my mother not know. She fusses enough as it is."

He shifted on his feet, uncomfortable with that request. "I report to your mother."

"Then I'm asking you to wait. Tell her at the end of the assignment, in whatever sort of debrief you have." She gave a shrug.

He sighed. "That's not the deal."

"Please, Jacob. She'll get upset and tell me to come home and this… This is my chance to really make a mark. Besides, I have you, right? I'll be fine. After all, there's no actual threat in the email."

"You are a stubborn, stubborn woman." He understood where she was coming from, but he had a job to do. "Listen, if you don't want me to send it to your IT people, will you let me send it to mine?" He'd been hired only as private security, but he had his own people. Besides, he seriously doubted the Aurora IT department had the same skill set as his cybersecurity team.

She hesitated, which he took as a good sign. "You'll send it there and keep Aurora out of it?"

He didn't like lying to her, so he prevaricated a little. "Your team doesn't need to know. And I'm sticking to you like glue from now on," he added.

Which was just lovely, wasn't it? Because he wanted to be close to her more than was proper. His thoughts had left proper behind ages ago.

"Then you'd better go get dressed. It's a tuxedo night. We need to leave in an hour."

He stared at her. "You can't mean you're still going to this party."

"Of course I am." She shut the lid on the laptop and put her hands on her hips. "I refuse to be intimidated. This is the biggest party of the week, far bigger than Aurora's tomorrow night. I'm not missing it, even if I am tired."

He shook his head. "Charlotte…"

"Don't Charlotte me. Intimidating me is exactly what this person wants. Well, I'm not so easily intimidated. I'm going to go in there, put on my killer dress, and we're going." She reached out and put her hand on his arm, and he tried not to stiffen even though his body was saying *danger*! "Whoever is doing this? I don't think they're going to be at this party tonight. It's very exclusive. And tomorrow there'll be pictures and whoever it is can choke on them for all I care."

She sounded brave and a bit reckless, but

he'd also seen her face when he'd arrived in the kitchen. She wasn't brushing it off. She was scared and she was being defiant. As long as she wasn't stupid, there was no reason why they couldn't go. After all, his job was protecting people who had enemies, who had to be in public situations.

"But if I say go, we go," he said, moving his arm away from her touch. It felt far too good.

"If you say go, we go," she parroted, nodding. "Go get ready, Jacob."

"As soon as I forward that email on to my guy." He gave a curt nod toward her laptop. "I could hack my way in, but if you'll bring up your email, it'll be faster."

He enjoyed the way her eyes widened with surprise and then appreciation. In moments she'd lifted the top again and logged in. "Go ahead. I trust you. See you when I'm ready."

She trusted him. She shouldn't. Because maybe he wasn't going to send the email to her IT team, but he was going to report what had happened to Aurora. It was his job, and despite his growing feelings, it was the one thing that kept him anchored. This was a job. That's all.

When he was done forwarding the email, he went to his room and got the tux out of the garment bag. Even though it was tailored perfectly to his frame, he never quite got used to the feel of formal wear. It took three separate tries to get the bow tie mostly right. His shoes were so shiny that the light reflected off them. He ran his fingers through his hair and sighed... It was time for a cut again, wasn't it? Was it too long now on the top?

Why was he being so critical of himself?

He was ready before she was, so he opened up his own laptop. The kind of messages that Charlotte was receiving weren't random, and while he was, on paper, just the hired protection, he had skills and resources. Including personnel files from Aurora. This felt to him like someone bearing a grudge. Someone who maybe worked for the company at one time. It wouldn't hurt to go through the team's files again and see if anything popped out.

Charlotte emerged twenty minutes later, and when Jacob turned around, he forgot about the file open on his laptop, forgot about his lopsided bow tie, forgot about everything.

Charlotte Pemberton was stunning.

Her dress was black, but looked like it had something underneath that was light beige, so the "feathers" of black fabric appeared to be over skin. The neckline plunged nearly to her waist, a deep V of creamy skin and shadows of cleavage that turned his mouth dry and his body hard. The "skirt" was more feathers of black, but then others that were iridescent, green and blue, like a peacock's feathers. It was daring and beautiful and unique. Just like her.

"Wow," he said, feeling like he should have been able to come up with a better word. "You weren't joking when you said you had a killer dress."

"You like it?" She turned in a circle, and the iridescent feathers shimmered. To his surprise, the back dipped nearly as low as the front.

He wanted to say he liked the woman inside it better, but held back. "It's beautiful."

She blushed a little. "Thank you. I hope you have your party shoes on, Jacob. I know I said I was tired, but the email fired me up. Now I want to dance out of spite."

"The best revenge is living well," he replied, "though I'm not sure you want me to dance."

"Hmm. We'll see."

She grabbed a soft wrap and their driver headed through the darkness toward Brooklyn and the A-list party. Jacob considered it a bad thing when he realized he felt like he was on a date rather than an assignment. He'd have to watch that through the night, but it was hard when the assignment was keeping his eyes on her and remaining glued to her side.

One thing he knew for sure… No one was going to hurt her. Not on his watch.

CHAPTER SEVEN

WEDNESDAY MORNING PROMISED a dawn that was crisp and clear. Charlotte was already up and doing battle with the nerves in her stomach. The Aurora show was at 10:00 a.m. and Amelie had left her messages last night with updates from the team, a few of them a little panicked. When Charlotte messaged back to apologize for the late reply but that she'd been out, Amelie had responded that she didn't realize Charlotte was going out. She should have; the party was on the itinerary for the week and hadn't changed.

"I'll meet you at eight thirty," Amelie had said, but Charlotte knew that things would be underway long before then. She trusted her team, but she also had the burning urge to make sure everything was going to plan. Which was why she'd been up for over an hour, had convinced Jacob to skip his workout, and they were ready to leave for Tribeca before 7:00 a.m.

Manhattan was already buzzing with traffic, the early morning energy palpable as they reached the venue. A security guard required ID before letting them through, and Charlotte took a moment to breathe in and absorb the moment, the quiet of the runway before the crowds entered and the music started.

Racks of clothing waited in the large, quiet room, and Charlotte paused inside the door, taking in the last moments of peace before everything went crazy. There was nothing like the energy before a big show. Now Aurora's best hung before her, waiting to be showcased by world-class models in one of the biggest shows in the world.

She stepped in, then hesitated. Something felt wrong. A scratch sounded close by, like a foot sliding against the floor. Jacob's hand touched her shoulder—he'd heard it, too.

She squinted and took a closer look at the nearest rack of clothes, and then her body ran cold.

They weren't hanging just right, and she realized with a start that the clothes were sliced, ruined. She moved out from beneath Jacob's hand and rushed to the rack, her fingers touching the rent fabric. "Oh, my God," she said, and then louder, "Oh, my God." Every item on the rack had been cut, and cut in such a way that they couldn't be repaired and certainly not before the show at ten.

"Stay here," Jacob ordered, and for once she did exactly what she was told. Both because she was shocked by what she was seeing and because of last night's email. Her dress had been slashed, and now all the items were cut to ribbons. Who would do something like this?

He scanned the room and then began to search. Once, she saw him stop and his head turn, and then suddenly he made a dash for the back of the room, where a door started to open before there was a loud thump.

"Drop the scissors," Charlotte heard him say, in a tone that sent shivers down her spine. She would never want to be on the receiving end of that sort of instruction. It was even different from the day she'd dashed to the deli for bagels, disobeying his orders.

She raced to where he was with whomever he'd caught...and stopped in absolute shock when she came face-to-face with Amelie, her wrists held firmly by Jacob.

Her assistant. Her confidante. The person she'd told about the earlier emails, had set up her itinerary, had been so sympathetic and... her friend.

Amelie had sabotaged today's show.

Charlotte wasn't sure if she was more angry

or hurt. Oh, she was furious at the sabotage, but she was also decimated by the betrayal. The Pembertons didn't let many people in, just by the nature of their money and fame. Trust was a rare commodity. To have hers violated in this way made her sick to her stomach.

"Why?" she asked, her voice raw around the massive lump in her throat. "Why would you do this?"

Jacob took the scissors from Amelie's grip and threw them on the floor. The venom that gleamed in Amelie's eyes was startling. "You really don't know. You sit in your office and make decisions and you don't give a damn how they affect people."

Confusion was added to the maelstrom of emotions flooding Charlotte. "What are you talking about?"

"I'm talking about Marie!" At Charlotte's still-confused look, Amelie spat, "Marie Tremblay!"

Now Charlotte understood. She nodded at Jacob, who released Amelie's wrists and took a step back, still staying between her and the discarded scissors. "Who is Marie to you? She was stealing from the company, Amelie."

"Who is she? *Mon Dieu*, you never paid any attention to my personal life at all. Never asked if I was dating, about my family… Marie is my girlfriend. She is a brilliant designer, but she never got the recognition she deserved. Always passed over. How else was she supposed to move up as a designer?" Amelie was nearly shouting. "You ruined her. No one will touch her now!"

Charlotte took a deep breath and pushed her feelings aside. "Marie stole designs from Aurora. She made her own decisions knowing full well there would be consequences if she were caught. Why send me the threatening emails, then? I had nothing to do with firing her."

"Because I had to see you every damn day, your smug face and not a care in the world, while our world was turned totally upside down."

Not a care? Charlotte fully acknowledged that her stressors were very much what people would call "first-world problems," but she had her own goals, dreams, insecurities, failures.

"And last night's email? Ugh, that's why you were surprised I went to the party, right? You figured I'd be too upset?"

"You went off the itinerary and went on that stupid shopping trip." She swore in French, making Charlotte's eyes widen. "That dress you wore? Do you know who designed it? Marie! And you had the nerve to wear it." Each word sounded dipped in poison.

That Amelie had held such hatred while pretending to be a loyal employee and friend felt unreal. Charlotte looked her in the eyes and said, "You're a very good actress, and maybe that can be a second career for you. Because you're obviously fired, Amelie."

"You could press charges, Charlotte." Jacob had remained quiet, but now spoke up. "She harassed and threatened you, and vandalized Aurora property."

"That's something I'll talk to Legal about." She met Jacob's eyes briefly, then looked at Amelie again. "Get out of here, check out of your hotel room and get the first flight home. And don't even try going to the office when you get back. We'll pack and send you your things."

"Charlotte…" That from Jacob.

"No, I mean it, Jacob. I want her out of my sight."

Amelie moved to leave, went by Charlotte and muttered, "Bitch."

When she was gone, Charlotte stood for a few moments, unsure what to do. "What do you need?" Jacob asked, after bending over to pick up the scissors Amelie had used to destroy months of work.

She couldn't deal with feelings right now; there was no time. "Amelie's security passes have to be revoked. I don't want her anywhere near anything to do with Aurora."

"I can look after that."

"The show is canceled. There's no way we can pull it off now." It cut her to the quick to say it. This show was to be her big chance to show everyone that she had what it took. She was supposed to step out into her own, really cement her value to the family business. Instead the whole thing was a failure.

But there wasn't time to let that get to her. "I'll cancel the show. Then everything here has to be boxed up and…" Her fingers trailed over a nearby gown. "And sent back. I want it all sent back home."

"All right. We'll work together to get it done." He smiled reassuringly and reached out to squeeze her arm. "By the way, you were fierce back there. Totally calm and self-possessed."

"It didn't feel like it."

"That's twice you've held your ground, Charlotte. You're stronger than you give yourself credit for," he answered, squeezing her arm again before going to meet with security.

The show was canceled, and the fashion division team that had come from Paris came to pack up the room. It was unusually quiet after Charlotte had spoken to them as one, praising their hard work, asking them to keep mum on the events of the day and allow Charlotte, and Aurora, time to issue an official statement.

It was bound to be a PR nightmare. Charlotte knew she'd be dealing with press releases and interviews and sound bites all week, but this… This was different. No one canceled shows during Fashion Week. Everyone would be after the scandalous details.

She had a brief video call with the family to update them on what was happening, saying she'd have an initial press release to send to them and Legal by noon. All the while Jacob was in the background, helping where he could. Including sending someone for coffee and blintzes from the same deli she'd gone to that first morning. It was a sweet gesture, and a warm spot in a cold, horrible day. He, too, was an Aurora employee, but he did something that he knew would make her feel cared for, and it nearly made her cry, if she hadn't had such a firm hold on her emotions.

They left the venue, doing their best to avoid the journalists who had already got wind of the story, and went back to the apartment, where Jacob made more coffee and put it at her elbow as she worked on a press release and sent it to Paris. Then she sat back and rubbed her eyes, exhausted. It had been five hours and it might as well have been fifteen. She felt as if she'd been run over by a truck.

This was supposed to be *the* day. A triumph. How had it come to this? All her plans and hopes crushed by one upset employee. How could Charlotte have been so blind?

Jacob came back into the dining room and put another mug by her elbow, but this time it was full of soup. "You need something to eat. You can't survive on coffee and half a blintz all day."

"You don't have to care for me so," she said softly. "But for the first time since I got on that plane last week, I'm truly very glad you're here."

"You lost the person you trusted most, and that leaves you feeling alone," he said, taking the seat beside her. His gray eyes delved into hers. "You totally sprang into action, but you've got to have some pretty heavy feelings about it all."

"I do. I'm not sure I'm ready to feel them yet. I'm still in crisis management mode."

"Fair."

"I wish my father were here." The words came out of nowhere, hitting her with a punch of emotion. "Dad always had a way of taking a bad situation and putting it in perspective. Or keeping things calm while we sorted out a plan."

"You still miss him."

"A lot. The family hasn't been the same since

he died. We're faking it a lot. But today… I'm not sure I have the energy to pretend."

"It's okay to still be sad. It's a testament to how much you loved him."

He was right. "I'm glad you're here, Jacob. Even if I don't need protecting anymore." She shook her head, still trying to wrap it around the fact that Amelie was behind it all. "Amelie wouldn't dare try anything now. I think she knows I would press charges. She'll go back to Paris with her tail between her legs."

Charlotte lifted the mug and sipped some of the flavorful broth. "Oh, that's perfect. Thank you." Then she looked at Jacob and sighed. "I just can't figure out what her end game was. What did she hope to achieve?"

"Ruining you, for a start. And once it was over, I bet she would have started looking for another job and quit. Her mission would have been accomplished, and she could have faded away without anyone suspecting. Consequence free."

"It seems like a pointless waste of time," Charlotte replied, sipping more soup. "The truth is, Marie deserved to be fired. It's not like we enjoyed it. She was a brilliant designer. Anyway, while I'm waiting for feedback on the press release, what are we supposed to do about the party tonight?"

"You haven't canceled it?"

She shook her head. "Amelie destroyed our clothing, but that's all. I think it should go ahead. One ruined show doesn't have to ruin everything." She smiled up at him. "I'm a bit stubborn that way."

"It's one of the things I've come to like about you," he admitted, his voice softer than she recalled it ever being before.

"My stubbornness?" she laughed.

"Yes." His gaze clung to hers now. "It made me pretty angry the first day, but last night, after getting that email... You were so determined to be unafraid and go on with your plans. Not in a foolish way, but in an I-refuse-to-be-intimidated way. I admire that."

"Well," she said, a little breathless, "imagine that. Jacob Wolfe actually admires something about me."

"More than one thing," he murmured, and she suddenly realized how close they were sitting. Not once had he acted inappropriately toward her, or touched her in any way that wasn't professional. The most he'd touched her all week was a hand at her back when they entered a room, and today when he'd gripped her arm. Now he wasn't touching her at all but oh, it felt as if he was, he was that close. Close enough she could reach out and touch him if she wanted.

What she really wanted was to rest her head on his shoulder for a few minutes and let the weight of the day fall away. It was only the feeling that she'd seem ridiculous that held her back.

And then he did the most amazing thing. He lifted his hand and placed it along the side of her face, a tender, reassuring touch that made her close her eyes with gratitude. She tried to remember the last time she got a really great bona fide hug and couldn't. If she had it was probably William or something, at Christmas.

As she leaned into his warm hand, she realized that she was incredibly touch-starved. A sigh escaped her lips as she let some of the stress of the day go.

"You're exhausted."

She opened her eyes and smiled a little. "Yes, but I still have enough energy to get through tonight. You'll still come, won't you?"

His gaze plumbed hers, asking silent questions.

"I want you to," she said. "Not as my bodyguard. As my guest, as a friend. I know I've been a pain in your neck sometimes this week, but it hasn't been all bad. And you've really come through when I needed it."

"*It hasn't been all bad.* High praise." But he smiled, the tiniest hint of a dimple creasing his cheek.

"Your tux was sent out for cleaning and should be back in your closet. And I think you'll like tonight's dress." She'd picked it out earlier in the week, eschewing the planned black-and-white number and instead going for something vibrant and very unmistakable. Janet had had it sent over yesterday, and it had been sitting in Charlotte's closet ever since. If this party was going to make a statement about Aurora, she was going to make a personal statement, too.

He brushed his fingers against her cheek. "I come from a different world," he replied. "One where it doesn't really matter what dress you wear. You're a beautiful woman, Charlotte. But that's not because of what you wear or how you do your hair or anything like that."

She figured that for a man like him, this was damned near poetic, and her heart softened even further. "So you'll come with me?"

He sighed. "Charlotte, I'm the wrong kind of man for you. I don't live in your world and to be honest, I don't want to. I'm a regular guy who knows nothing about fashion. Money doesn't change who I am. Deep down I'm still a soldier. A plain, ordinary grunt who would never fit in with your movie stars and models and moguls."

"Did you consider those are the exact reasons I like you?" She put her hand over his, still on her cheek. "I know you're not with me because of what you'll gain from it. It's refreshing."

"I have no idea why you trust me."

She looked in his eyes. "Because you have not given me a reason not to. Because I'm not twenty-two and naive anymore." She turned her face and kissed his palm, a tiny press of her lips. "Before the party last night…what you said… I don't think I'm the only one who's had their heart broken. And I'm sorry, Jacob. I'm sorry you've been hurt so badly."

His throat bobbed. "This is so far over the professional line," he murmured.

"It's over. There doesn't have to be a professional line anymore. So come with me tonight. As my friend. Please."

"I'll come with you."

She smiled, suddenly energized again, knowing she wouldn't have to walk into that ballroom alone. "Thank you. Let's get ready and show the world that the Pembertons don't stay down for long. We might have canceled the show, but Aurora will go on long after today."

He stood and held out his hand. She took it and rose from her chair, then gave it a small squeeze before letting go and heading to her room.

One thought kept running through her brain: Jacob wasn't an Aurora employee anymore. Tonight, everything could change.

CHAPTER EIGHT

JACOB COULDN'T TAKE his eyes off her.

Gone was the trademark black-and-white couture, and in its place was a stunning gown in a vivid, hot pink, the perfect color for her creamy skin and dark hair. From the moment she'd stepped out of her room he'd been mesmerized, and that was saying something. Jacob Wolfe didn't do mesmerized. Not anymore. And yet now, as he held a glass of Scotch in his hand and watched her talking half a room away, he was entranced.

His mission was accomplished. He could go home in three days as scheduled, Charlotte was safe, the mystery of the emails solved, everything back to normal. Just the way he wanted. He could take his trip to Tenerife. Exactly right. Then he'd return and continue running a company that protected VIPs and dignitaries and made him a truckload of money.

Except then Charlotte turned a half turn and

looked over her shoulder at him, and he was
sunk. She smiled, and he wondered what the
hell he was going to do.

Go home and forget about her, that's what.
He'd spoken the truth earlier. He wasn't the man
for her. Hell, even being here tonight he was
a complete fish out of water. As a bodyguard
he stayed in the background, on the perimeter
of the high-powered worlds of his clients. He
was…in his place. This, though, was different.
He was faking his way through the evening,
but it wasn't fitting right. Kind of like having
a sock wrinkle under your foot and not being
able to adjust your shoe to fix it.

He finished off the Scotch—his liquid cour-
age—as Charlotte wound her way through the
crush of people to where he waited. He didn't
mind the tux; he was used to being in formal
wear and the Hackett suit had been tailored spe-
cifically for him. The bow tie felt constrictive as
he swallowed. All he could think of was that he
wasn't Charlotte's bodyguard any longer. That
barrier between them was gone, and there was
no denying they'd been fighting an attraction
to each other all week. How could he not be attracted to her? She was beautiful, smart and
brave. Not once had she cowered when it came
to the harassment leveled at her. If anything,
she'd stepped up her game. God, how he ad-

mired that. No matter how far apart they were in social spheres, he was still attracted to her. Uncomfortably so.

She stood in front of him now, in that pink column of fabric that clung to her curves, enveloping her breasts in a strapless neckline that looked like a heart. The small train behind gave her such a Hollywood glamour look that he was sure she was something out of a dream.

"You're bored," she announced, her eyes twinkling.

"I swear I'm not." He wasn't, either. He was busy keeping his eyes on her. Not because he was paid to, but because he couldn't help himself.

The ballroom glittered around them, all chandeliers and gilt and sparkly dresses and jewels and fashion royalty. It was a very different feel from the sometimes raucous party they'd gone to last night, but it fit Charlotte, fit the Aurora brand. Champagne flowed and wait staff circulated with delicacies for nibbling. Instead of the hip-hop artist from the Brooklyn warehouse, the music was provided by a classics crooner even Jacob recognized.

Class. That was Aurora and that was Charlotte, all the way. He was so out of his league. He was a cop's son who grew up on beans on toast and then moved to the army where the food was, if not better, more plentiful. Charlotte, though not a snob, had been raised with the proverbial silver spoon in her mouth.

Why was he thinking this way, anyway? He needed to walk away, and soon.

"Come on, Jacob. I think we should dance."

His blood warmed even as the denial sprang to his lips. "Are you sure that's a good idea?"

She grabbed his hand. "You're not my bodyguard anymore. Tonight you're my guest. There are no rules, nor protocols or ethics to follow."

"What about my personal code?"

She put her free hand on her hip. "Does that code include turning down a woman in the most fabulous dress ever? Because if it does, I don't like your code."

He nearly laughed, then gave in. "All right. I'll dance with you." Not like it was a hard choice anyway. The chance to hold her in his arms was too sweet to resist. *Just this once*, he told himself.

She led him to the floor in front of the small stage and he tugged on her hand, deftly pulling her into his arms. He wasn't a great dancer, but he could be smooth if he kept the steps simple. Her eyes widened in surprise at the first contact, then warmed as she melted into his embrace. The scent of her—something slightly floral— wrapped around him. It was February, a month of white and gray and brown in New York, but Charlotte was as beautiful and alive as an English country spring.

He turned her to the music and realized what a sappy thing he'd just thought.

"You're a good dancer," she said, close to his ear. The crazy-high heels she wore brought her closer to his height, and the way their bodies brushed lit him on fire.

"I'm adequate at best," he replied, keeping his hand appropriately at the curve of her back, no lower.

She turned her head so their gazes met. "You're more than adequate, Jacob. This week you've put up with me and you've been so supportive, when I know that isn't in your job description. I just want to say thank you. For going above and beyond."

"You are far from my most challenging assignment," he murmured. "It was my pleasure."

"Oh, don't say that. Not pleasure. Not when…"

Her voice trailed off, and warning bells went off in his head. The music carried on but now every point at which their skin touched, electricity shot between them. "Charlotte," he warned.

"Don't." Her eyes flashed at him. "Don't say you don't feel it, too, because I know you do."

He couldn't deny it.

And there were too many reasons why he

couldn't—shouldn't—let this go any further, but he couldn't say them here, not at a crowded party, not while dancing. He would do it when they were alone. As they would be later. In the same Manhattan apartment, and in separate bedrooms.

"Jacob," she whispered. He barely heard her but he saw her lips move.

He had seen his name on someone else's lips like that before, and the pain of it struck him right in the heart, a cold dagger of regret.

The circumstances were different, but a man didn't get over losing someone they loved so easily. Charlotte was not in mortal danger. She was not taking crazy risks as an informant. But Jacob had been responsible for Jacinta's death. He knew better than to let his success go to his head. He was a simple guy with a lot of flaws, who sucked at personal relationships, and he had no business thinking about a woman like Charlotte Pemberton in that way.

"You went somewhere," she said, drawing him back into the present even though his feet hadn't stopped moving. "Where?"

"Nowhere you'd care to go," he replied, his voice hardening.

"Are you sure?" She tried a smile, but her eyes were soft. "It's okay, Jacob."

"What's okay?"

Her fingers trailed over his shoulder. "To feel this way. To…want what you think you can't have."

"Charlotte." She was so close to propositioning him and he knew he needed to say no but didn't want to. He thought of the butterfly necklace sitting back in his drawer, thought about how the colors would have looked tonight against her skin and with the bright hue of her gown. Whatever had happened this week had made her come out of her cocoon, hadn't it? The woman in his arms right now was Charlotte Pemberton. She wasn't Aurora Germain's daughter or the company PR spokesperson. She was her own woman, on her own terms. And she was, for all intents and purposes, articulating that she wanted to be with him.

As if she could sense his inner battle, she stepped away when the song ended. "Come, let's get another drink."

They weaved their way through the crowd to the bar, where she ordered a gin and tonic and he ordered another Scotch. Drinks in hand, she lifted her glass in a toast and touched it to his. "To Amelie being back in France, and Aurora for being the bastion of fashion."

"Nicely put," he agreed, tapping the glass against hers. "The press release was very well done, by the way. Aurora's worth doesn't rely on one trip down the runway."

"Exactly. What happened was horrible. Months of work had gone into that line, but the line still exists. We spin it to our advantage. Maybe Amelie wanted to ruin us, but if we play it right, this gives us more publicity and a news cycle that we can exploit." She took a healthy sip of her drink. "Better yet, Amelie can't give interviews about it, since she signed a nondisclosure agreement. She speaks, and we'll see her in court."

"You're ruthless," he said, meaning it as a compliment.

"I have a lot of Maman in me. But I'm also just me. Tired of black and white. Ready to take on the fight myself." She smiled suddenly, so bright it lit the room. "Oh, Jacob, I came here to make my mark and find a way to take my place in the company. I thought it was by running a flawless week just like Maman would. How wrong I was! It's dealing with this crisis that has given me confidence and assurance. I feel wonderful!"

He chuckled. "You feel about three drinks in."

She laughed. "Maybe. But it's our party. Look at the crowd! Aurora is as strong as ever, and

I'm proud to be a part of it. Not as Aurora Germain's daughter, but as Charlotte Pemberton."

Who was he to put the brakes on this moment? Maybe he didn't get fashion but he did understand the rush she was feeling, the victory. When the *Vogue* columnist from earlier in the week appeared, he stepped back and let Charlotte step into the spotlight.

Saturday. Saturday was his flight to Paris, though maybe he could rebook and go straight to London. Maybe he could fly out tomorrow sometime and remove himself from the temptation of her. Or he could stay and...

Stay and let Charlotte take the lead. They both knew that in the end he'd go back to his life and she'd return to hers. As long as they both knew the score and consented, no one would get hurt.

He wouldn't make the mistake of making promises, that was for sure. Not again. No promises, no risk.

Just two days with Charlotte. Did he dare?

Charlotte rode up in the elevator with Jacob, her head clear. She'd switched to sparkling water after she'd talked with Lauralea from *Vogue*, wanting to be sober and in possession of all her faculties when she dealt with Jacob and what was going to happen between them.

She was sure now that he wanted it as much as she. The air in the elevator was heavy, and she was warm beneath the toasty wrap she wore over her dress. But now that they were alone together, conversation had disappeared. She wasn't sure what to say. Maybe once they were in the apartment together...

The elevator doors slid open, nearly silent in the empty corridor. Jacob stepped out and then put his hand against the sliding door to ensure it stayed open as she exited the car. His face was so serious right now. The fun and levity of the party had fled once they left the hotel and got in the limousine.

Her hand shook as she entered the security code for the apartment, then stepped inside.

The foyer was dark, and soft light from the living room beckoned them in. Before Charlotte could move, though, Jacob was there, easing the wrap off her shoulders. The air was cool on her skin, and she broke out in goose bumps. But Jacob merely dropped her wrap on a small table and put his hands on her shoulders. His wide, warm, slightly rough hands.

He was touching her, finally. She drew in a shaky breath, wanting to prolong the moment, yet wanting to turn around and launch herself into his arms.

"Charlie," he murmured, and a full-on shiver

erupted down her body as his warm breath touched behind her ear just before his lips touched the skin of her neck ever so softly.

Charlie. No one had ever given her a nickname before. She had always been fully Charlotte. The sound of it was strange to her ears, but so very welcome. It was fun and a little quirky and made her feel just a bit special.

"Mmm." She arched her neck, making room for his lips, and he didn't disappoint. Her nipples hardened into points at the light, seductive contact. He ran a finger just behind her ear, holding her hair back so he could access the tender skin better. A gasp escaped her lips as his tongue touched her earlobe. And yet all contact was slow and perhaps even a bit hesitant. Testing.

She swallowed tightly as he made no further move, because she understood what he was asking. He'd made his play, but he was waiting for consent. For reciprocation. Her heart tumbled at the knowledge. Jacob Wolfe was perhaps the most ethical man she'd ever met. He spoke to her plainly, without worry about her feelings or coming off well. Just honesty and a trust that she could take whatever he was going to say. He treated her…as an equal.

Today she might have crawled into a hole and cried about what had happened with the show. Instead she'd stood tall and carried on. Jacob had said he admired that. Now he was nuzzling her neck and she had never in her life felt more empowered than she did at this moment.

She turned around so that she was facing him, and met his gaze. The gray of his eyes was like lightning, full of need and restrained power. That he was capable of such gentleness was seductive in itself.

"Kiss me," she whispered.

"You're sure this is what you want?"

She nodded. "You're not my bodyguard anymore, Jacob. You're just a man. A man I've wanted to kiss for days. Please don't make me wait any longer."

She'd expected something grand and passionate, something that burned hot and incinerated her into ash. She didn't expect the tender way he cupped her face in his large hands, or stared into her eyes as he lowered his head. His lashes went down and she got a glimpse of their sandy color before she closed her eyes, too, and his lips touched hers.

It was gentle, reverent, decimating.

His mouth moved over hers, sampling, tasting, making her feel cherished and loved and hungry for so much more. She put her hands under his overcoat and pushed it off his shoulders and to the floor; neither of them cared that it dropped in a black heap of fabric. He'd looked so devastating in his tuxedo, and as he kissed her long and deep, she reached for the bow tie and released it, dropping the strip of silk on top of his coat. Then the tux jacket, the fine threads of it beneath her fingers, was discarded, too. His hands rested on her ribs, but she pressed up against him, feeling his taut, strong body, reaching for his hand and placing it on her breast.

"Charlotte," he gasped, sliding his mouth off hers. "This is—"

"Charlie," she said firmly. "I liked it when you called me that."

"Charlie…" Her name sounded on a sigh. He ran his lips over her jaw and she shivered again, with anticipation and desire. "We should talk about this…what we expect…"

She reached up and placed her hands on either side of his face, forcing him to look at her. "I don't want a bloody contract, Jacob. I only have one expectation, and that is for you to please rock my world."

"That's a very clear affirmative."

"Yes, soldier, it is. I want you. And I don't want you to hold back." Even as she said it, she had a hard time believing it was her. Where had this self-assured, adventurous woman come from? She was a rule follower. Tonight she was breaking the rules, and it felt glorious. The idea of Jacob giving her everything made her tremble. Was she ready for that? To possess and be possessed? She wasn't sure she wouldn't be overwhelmed, but for once in her life she wanted to stop doing a risk analysis in her brain every time she made a decision. She was tired of giving up what she wanted for the greater good.

She didn't expect him to lift her up into his strong arms, and she gave a little squeak as she clung to his neck. He started down the hall and stopped at his room, not hers, and she wondered why. But there was little time to ask because he kicked the door shut with his foot and then let her down beside the king-size bed.

Without saying a word, he released the cuffs of his shirt, then the buttons down the front, pulling out the tails and letting the fine fabric gape open, revealing a slice of muscled chest. Slowly, so slowly it was painfully magnificent, he shrugged out of the shirt and tossed it aside to the tufted chair nearby.

"You're beautiful," she said, her body clamoring for his touch. She stepped forward, only two steps, and that put him in reach. She could see him better in the soft light cast by the lamp, and she noticed his imperfections. Dimpled scars, one at his right shoulder, another by his ribs. A slightly pink one just below his navel, maybe three, four inches long. "Your history," she remarked quietly, putting her finger on one of the scars.

"I'm not easy to get rid of," he replied, the flash of a grin curving his lips.

"I'm glad." Truthfully, the battle scars turned her on even more. "Will you tell me about them some time?"

His smile faded, and his gaze delved into hers. "Maybe," he said, and she realized that how he'd been injured was probably a source of pain and possibly anguish, and her question had been insensitive. He was entitled to his secrets, wasn't he? Just as she was entitled to hers. She traced her finger over the scar low on his belly, then ran her fingertips up his abdomen to his chest, leaning in to kiss the hard plane of muscle.

He reached behind her and found the zip of her dress, then lowered it, inch by inch, to her tailbone.

"Did I tell you how stunning you looked tonight?" he murmured, his voice husky. "This dress, and your smile… It took my breath away."

His sweet declaration was taking her breath away. She stepped back and shimmied out of the dress, leaving a pink puddle of skirt on the floor with the more structured bodice lying stiffly on top. She still wore the four-inch hot pink heels, but nothing else. Panty lines would have shown through the delicate material.

"My God," he breathed.

"I'm yours tonight."

Everything moved faster then, as if the urgency couldn't be held back any longer. He stepped forward and pulled her into his arms, his hands skimming over her body, weakening her knees and clouding her brain with nothing but dizzying sensation. She reached for the button of his trousers and they scrambled to remove the rest of his clothes, until they were both naked and dying to be closer.

"Leave your shoes on," he said roughly, as she perched on the edge of the bed. "They're the sexiest shoes I've ever seen." The hungry look in his eyes told her she was about to have her world rocked just as she'd asked.

He lay beside her on the duvet, his mouth plundering hers and then skittering down to her breasts. Her back arched instinctively, moving toward the contact, while his hand slid lower, turning her into a wanton puddle of need and desire. She surrendered completely, trusting him enough to lose herself in the heightened sensations he elicited from every nerve ending. But when she was gasping and close to her peak, she reached for him and he paused.

"I don't have a condom," he said, stilling and looking into her eyes.

Frustration bubbled through her arousal. "I don't, either. I didn't expect…"

"Nor did I."

"We could… I mean…" She lifted her hips, moaning as she pressed against his hand. "I don't want to stop, Jacob."

His breath accelerated. "Me, either. But I want you to be safe…"

"I am safe." She wrapped her hand around him.

"I can pull out."

That one suggestion—risky though it was—was enough for Charlotte to make up her mind. She trusted him to do what he said. And she had never wanted anyone as much as she wanted him right now. Hadn't she just thought that she wanted to stop all the risk analysis?

"Yes," she whispered. "Yes, Jacob. Don't stop."

CHAPTER NINE

CHARLOTTE WOKE FROM a deep, satisfied sleep. The lamp beside the bed was still on, and she eased herself over and quietly reached for it, flicking the switch and casting the room in darkness. Jacob's breathing was steady and even, and she curled back under the covers where it was warm from their body heat.

"What time is it?" he asked softly.

"I don't know. I didn't want to wake you. Sorry."

"Don't be sorry. Come here." He opened his arm and she snuggled against him, both of them naked as the day they were born.

They were quiet for a few minutes and then Jacob said, "Are you okay? After last night?"

She nodded against the hollow of his shoulder. "Are you?"

He chuckled. "Takes more than a little thing like you to mess me up."

She couldn't help the smile that spread on

her face. "That's not what I meant." Neither of them had been gentle, but that hadn't been what they wanted, either. Heat crept up Charlotte's cheeks when she thought of how open and vocal she'd been.

He kissed the top of her head. "I know. Sorry if making a joke wasn't appropriate."

She shrugged. "We left inappropriate behind a long time ago, didn't we?"

He sighed. "Yeah. I guess we did."

"We should probably talk about what happens now, though." She expected his muscles to tense, but he stayed relaxed against her. "I mean first off, one of us needs to go to the drugstore today and get protection."

He laughed, his chest rising and falling abruptly. "Damn, Charlie, that was not what I expected you to say."

She loved the sound of his laugh, the way it rumbled up through his chest. "Well, we're here until Saturday. And I don't think it's realistic to think we won't be doing this again."

"Fair." His hand trailed over her arm. "There's no denying we have chemistry."

Chemistry, she thought, but not love. Then again, they had known each other just under a week. Love would be impossible. And a lie, too, wouldn't it? No one fell in love that quickly.

She thought of her brother, William, and his

fiancé, Gabi. Well, maybe. But they were definitely the exception.

"Right," she finally answered. "But after that…"

"I go back to London and my job, and you go back to Paris, and we look back at this as a very interesting week in our histories."

He was so right, and it was exactly what she had been planning to say, so why did she feel so deflated?

She was quiet for so long that he nudged her with his arm. "Does that disappoint you?"

"Yes. And I don't know why, because it was what I was thinking, too. It's for the best, right?"

He shifted so he was on his side, facing her. She could barely make out his features in the dark; the curtains in the window let in very little of the city lights and his face was wrapped in gray shadows. "Charlotte, I'm not made for relationships, and I don't belong in your world. You should know that before you decide if things go any further between us this week. It's not fair for me to give you any hope if that's what you're looking for."

"I'm not!" She rose up on one elbow, her feelings crowding around her, confusing. "God, maybe it's just the craziness of this week jumbling everything up. I knew last night that this would be a no-strings thing. I went into it with my eyes open. But so much has happened… Maybe I'm more of a mess than I realized."

"You're talking to the champ on that one."

"No doubt."

But she didn't press. Didn't want to. It wasn't a stretch to believe that he had his own demons to vanquish.

He waited a few moments, then put his hand, so warm and comforting, on her hip. "This thing with Amelie… It's affected you deeply."

She nodded. "Very." Dare she share with him, even though she didn't expect the same in return? Perhaps it was safe this way. She trusted him, and when they went their own ways it wouldn't matter, would it? Plus it would be so good to unload a little without fear of burdening family.

"I have betrayal issues. Or rather, I question people's motives. It's what happens when you grow up as we all did. People always want something, even if it's just to be in the same picture frame with you. They want a job or a perk or to be your BFF. They make you believe they really care for you when really, they're just using you to lift their own profile. It's hard to believe people are genuine."

"I never thought you might be a cynic." His thumb rubbed circles on her hip and it felt heavenly. "But I guess I can see that. Mark What's-His-Name being a prime example."

"Exactly. I am the daughter of an earl, and now my brother is an earl. That alone put us in certain circles. But then, with the success of Aurora, it's a whole other plane of celebrity. I'm not complaining. It's such a first-world problem to have, really. But after being burned a few times, I'm careful who I trust."

"Burned?"

"A few friends when I was younger. And…a couple of boyfriends." The sting was still present. "I wasn't in love with them, but I liked them a lot. And then, yes, Mark. My track record is not great, so lately I've just…given up."

"And have been lonely."

Her breath caught. "Yes."

"Which is why this thing with Amelie is so hard."

"Exactly."

"And yet you trust me."

She thought about that for a few moments. "There's nothing you can possibly want from me now. We're too different. We live utterly different lives from each other. And if I can't trust someone who is hired to protect people for a living, then I might as well give up altogether. Your whole career is based on trust."

Though he didn't move, she felt as if he somehow withdrew after that last sentence. She reached over and smoothed her thumb over his cheekbone. "I said something wrong, didn't I?"

"Of course not."

"No, I did. You pulled away just now. Mentally. You don't have to tell me. I'm just sorry. I didn't mean to say anything to upset you."

Jacob's throat bobbed as he swallowed. He'd never wanted to tell anyone about Jacinta before, but he felt as if strong-but-gentle Charlotte might understand. A rock of regret settled in his stomach as he spoke. "You said my career is based on trust. You've never been more right. As an SAS team member, and as a security company, trust is paramount. It's just that once I broke one of the rules. It's a hard thing to get past. I'm not sure I ever will. Or if I should."

"No one's perfect, Jacob. It's unrealistic to expect it of yourself."

"But when someone like me isn't perfect, people can die." The words sounded strangled, as if they were having a hard time coming out of his mouth. "People have died." Grief welled up in him, feelings he kept trying to move past but never quite succeeding.

She stilled. "I'm so sorry."

"I don't talk about it."

She began moving her thumb again, and the soft, circular motion began to relax him the tiniest bit. He'd gone so tense beside her, his muscles bunched tightly, his jaw clenched. This was what he resisted, always. Someone feeling sorry for him, when he didn't deserve it. And then the revulsion when they inevitably realized his irresponsibility had caused a death. Sex with Charlotte was one thing. This shared-intimacy thing, though… It was too much. He shifted and went to get out of the bed when she stopped him with a firm grip on his arm.

"Maybe you should," she advised gently, "with someone who has no stake in it. With someone who is willing to listen without judgment. I can tell it's eating you up inside."

He sat back, bracing his back against the headboard. "That's just the thing, though. If I open up to you, you will judge me. I don't know how you couldn't."

"So you've never talked about this with anyone?"

Her question was met with silence.

"But that's not good for you. Having it fester all this time." She sat up beside him, faced him and arranged the bedding so she was covered. "Jacob, this whole week you've been my safe space. Let me be yours."

It was such a tempting offer. He hadn't leaned

on anyone in so long. He hadn't wanted to talk about it with his dad, and he'd lost touch with a lot of guys from the Special Forces community. The ones he hired as security experts... Well, they didn't dig into each other's business. "It's not easy for me."

"I know it's not. But you should share it with someone."

He hesitated a long time, unsure of what to do. The desire to finally talk about it pressed against him, though fear and revulsion held him back. He could still see it all in his mind like it was yesterday. Hear it. Smell it. His mouth tasted bitter and he swallowed, hoping to rid his tongue of the taste. It didn't work.

But Charlotte had his hands in hers and he let out a breath. "It was a while ago, just before I left the military. Our team was on an assignment in South America... I can't say where. But we were there for a while. Long enough that we'd established some informants from within the locals."

"There was a lot of danger?"

"There's always the potential of it, yeah. I was there to do a job. But then I met Jacinta."

He couldn't even say her name without feeling waves of love, regret, self-loathing.

"What happened to her?"

He had been staring straight ahead, but forced

himself to meet her gaze. Even in the dim light, he saw compassion and acceptance and wondered how on earth he'd ended up sharing a week with an angel. That's what she was, really. Take away the money and the fancy clothes, and the powerful friends... She was still a sweet, loving, strong person. Certainly not the princess he'd thought he'd be babysitting.

"It's okay if you can't," she whispered, squeezing his fingers. "You're under no obligation to tell me. I don't want to hurt you, Jacob."

Was she even real?

"I let myself get distracted," he said. "I forgot to do my job. And it got her killed."

The familiar emptiness opened up inside him, and to his shame tears stung the backs of his eyes. He'd held Jacinta's limp body in his arms, nearly lost his mind at the sight of her wounds and lifeless eyes.

"She loved you, too?"

He nodded. Jacinta had loved him, he was in no doubt of that. "I was so stupid. Promised her I'd take her back with us. Everything I knew better than to do." He rested his head against the headboard. "I put our whole team at risk, too. That's when I knew I'd had enough. It was time for me to retire. I had her death on my hands. I didn't want to have anyone else's."

She was quiet for a long time, and his confession settled around them. "But then you went into private security."

He nodded. "It's my skill set. I'm good at it. Some of the guys… They like the longer assignments. But I can do anything from a few hours to a few weeks. And to be honest, right or not, most of my clientele are middle-aged to old men."

She snorted. "Long live the patriarchy."

He chuckled then. "I love your sass, you know that?"

"I'm glad."

He reached out and pulled her close. "Charlie, I've never told anyone all that. How I cared for her and how I lost my edge. I'm trusting you to keep my confidence."

"Of course I will." Her fingers threaded with his now. "Jacob, at some point you're going to have to forgive yourself. You can't punish yourself for the rest of your life."

"Can't I?" He certainly deserved no better.

"You absolutely can, you're right. But it's no way to live. You deserve some happiness."

The bitter taste was back. "I'm pretty sure I don't. After all, Jacinta will never be happy. Her family will always miss her. What right do I have to be happy?"

"But you can't go on that way!" She rose to her knees and moved closer, then surprised him by grabbing his face with both hands. "If she loved you she would want you to go on and be happy. Not live in a constant state of guilt." She kissed his forehead, and his heart lurched. "You can't set an impossible expectation for yourself and then hate yourself for not reaching it. No one can attain perfection. Everyone in the world has some regret. And yeah, maybe yours is a big one. But God, Jacob. You're redeemable. Why can't you see that?"

He didn't know what to say. No one in his life had ever taken his side like this before, ever championed him unconditionally even knowing what he'd done. He was speechless for a few minutes, while she kissed his forehead again and ran her fingers through his hair.

It felt so good, her touch. It had been a long time since he'd had this kind of connection with anyone, and it scared the hell out of him even as it felt amazing. It felt like…hope. But he didn't want hope, did he? Especially when it was such a seductive feeling. Hope existed for only a short time and then it was quashed. He wasn't sure he'd make it through another death of hope again.

And yet… Charlotte. Charlie. He should send her to her room right now and make sure this never happened again. Instead his starved soul reached out to her and clung, wanting just a few more minutes of false salvation.

Her lips went to his mouth again and he tasted her, hungry for more of her pureness, her undaunted optimism. She kissed him back, fully, completely, her warm, soft body curling against his. They shouldn't make love again, not without protection. But that didn't mean he couldn't pleasure her, make sure she felt desired and cherished and, hell, satisfied.

When she called out his name in the dark, he knew he was in trouble. He'd care about it later.

Charlotte promised herself she wasn't going to look at Jacob any differently after the late-night confessions, but she couldn't help it. She'd bet anything that he hadn't realized there'd been tears on his cheeks when he'd told her about Jacinta. That he'd trusted her with such a traumatic secret was monumental. And yet, as she set about making coffee, she knew that their relationship—what there was of it—was going to be short-lived. Even if their lives weren't completely different, Jacob was not in any way ready for a relationship. For one, she was sure he still loved this Jacinta woman. Her death and his self-blame assured that there wouldn't be room for anyone else until he found a way to put it in the past.

She poured water over the grounds in the press and sighed. The kicker was that she wouldn't care for him as much if he were different. His pain showed a depth of feeling she couldn't ever remember seeing in any other man, other than her father. Her throat tightened. After having her heart broken, it had been her father, Cedric, who had dried her tears and then given her the support to stand tall again. Oh, how she missed him. Perhaps this week hadn't just been about Fashion Week. It had also been the result of years and months of stress—to live up to her father's faith in her, to do right by the business. What would Cedric say now?

He'd tell her to give herself a break, she realized, and could almost hear his voice in her head. The realization brought with it a small wave of grief, though these days the memories filled her heart rather than leaving her bereft. Time did heal, it seemed.

"Good morning."

She jumped at the sound of his voice behind her. "It's nearly noon. Not really morning anymore."

He looked down at his watch and swore. "But your itinerary…"

She laughed at the expression on his face. "Screw my itinerary. I took the morning off. I only have today and tomorrow anyway and then it's back to Paris. This morning I'm having coffee and taking my time with it. Then I'm going to go meet with the Paris team. They're flying back tomorrow and then taking a week of vacation. They worked extremely hard only to have their efforts ruined."

"They must be disappointed."

"And angry," she added. "Rightly so. They need to know they are valued and that their places are secure at Aurora."

"That's not a PR person job." He went to get a mug as she pressed down the plunger in the coffee press.

"No, but I'm the Aurora representative that's here. And maybe I do PR but I'm also invested in their success."

His smile widened. "You sounded like your mother just then."

"Imperative and regal?"

"Just so." He came closer, looped an arm around her waist and tugged her against his body. "And beautiful. And kind."

"My mother *is* kind. Though not many realize it."

"That bit was a guess for me, but I'm glad to hear it." He looked down into her eyes. "I've told myself a million times I shouldn't do this. That it can't go anywhere." He nuzzled at her cheek, sending a thrill down her spine.

"It doesn't have to go anywhere. It can stay right here in New York." She lifted her chin, rubbing her face against his soft, warm lips. "We have two days. I know you're not looking for anything...permanent. And neither am I. My schedule isn't exactly conducive to a relationship. And we live in different cities..."

"And in different worlds," he added, sliding his mouth over to her earlobe. For a second, she forgot how to breathe.

"How could you be so damned stoic all week? How could you stay so *I'm here to do a job* when you're so sexy underneath all that professionalism?"

"I'm off the clock now. Not working. I can be stoic if you want, though. Might be fun."

Her whole body was humming now, loving this freer side of him. "Hmm, maybe later. First, let's have coffee."

She poured both cups, and he fixed hers the way she liked. After only a few days, he'd remembered that little detail. They took their coffee into the living room, where they could look out over Central Park and what was, in her mind, the most beautiful part of Manhattan.

He'd taken several sips before he let out a breath and said, "The right thing for me to do would be to hop on a plane. My job is done and it wouldn't look right for me to stay."

She eyed him over the rim of her cup. "You don't strike me as the kind of man who worries about appearances." She'd half expected him to say such a thing, though. To feel the need to run. What had happened between them—the talking as much as the sex—had to have freaked him out. It was freaking her out a little, too.

"My professional reputation—"

She held up a hand. "Be honest. Your self-preservation is at work here, not concern for your reputation."

He coughed and she was glad she'd spoken up. No matter how they left things, she would know she'd been honest with him.

"Do you always say exactly what you think?"

"Of course not. I'm in PR. I hardly ever say what's really on my mind." And then she grinned at him.

"I guess it's just with me, then."

She thought about that and wondered if he wasn't on to something. She was known for being blunt but that wasn't the same as being honest. "Maybe," she admitted. "I've been saying what my family has wanted to hear about a lot of things, I think. Or if not, just kind of… following along."

"You made a statement this week, that's for sure. But truly, Charlotte. It might be best if I go."

She met his gaze. "Are you worried about me

getting ideas? That if you stay the two days, that if we spend those days together, I'll somehow magically think we are meant to be together forever and fall head over heels in love with you?"

To her surprise, he blushed.

"I won't," she said firmly. "Like we said earlier. We have different lives. And what you shared with me last night... I'm honored that you did that. But it also shows me that you're not in a place where a relationship is on the table. My eyes are open, Jacob. That being said..." She put her cup down on a small table and leaned forward, her elbows resting on her knees. "It's been a long time since I've liked someone, trusted someone. Heck, it's been a very long time since I had sex. Forgive me for wanting another forty-eight hours before having to give that up."

He relaxed his shoulders and let out a breath. "I don't want to go, either. Even if I should. But you have to know that this is all I have to give, Charlie."

"I know. I won't ask for more. I promise."

"Two days."

"Not even. I do still have some obligations. But definitely two more nights. And then Saturday we'll fly out together. And we'll say goodbye, with a smile."

She wasn't quite sure if she could pull off a

genuine smile at saying goodbye. In just a week he'd made such an impression on her heart. But she'd fake it if she had to, and keep the memory close as "that one time I had a fling with my bodyguard." It was best for everyone.

CHAPTER TEN

SATURDAY AFTERNOON THEY boarded a flight from New York to Paris. Ensconced in ultracomfortable first-class seats, Jacob indulged in a whiskey while Charlotte got a glass of white wine from the flight attendant. They toasted each other by clinking glasses, then Jacob took a sip of his drink. Sipping was important. Otherwise he'd find himself ordering another, and another. He wasn't looking forward to saying goodbye to Charlotte at the airport in Paris, where he'd catch a quick connection to London.

She'd kept her bargain to the letter. No request for promises or declarations of affection. It had been two days of enjoying each other. Sex, certainly, that blew his mind and made him incapable of moving his limbs for a good thirty minutes. But more than that. He still accompanied her to her work functions, and watched as she worked a crowded room, or spoke to a single person and made them feel as if they had her complete attention. He listened to her on a call with her family, going through business details about the fashion industry that blew his mind. She was so freaking smart.

And then there'd been the talks. Talks about their childhoods, which were so very different. And not just because of money, but because he'd been an only child while she'd had siblings. He'd told her about losing his mother to cancer when he wasn't even a teenager, and she told him about her father's death almost two years ago, and how decimated the family had been to lose Cedric.

Somewhere in those two days, he'd fallen for her. Hard.

Exhaustion swept over him, and he closed his eyes. Maybe he should fight to stay awake, spend every last second he could with her, but something had switched in his brain the moment they'd stepped on the plane. A signal that what had been their magical time was over now. The flight was just a kind of limbo between one world and the next.

Back to Wolfe Security. Back to London, and his flat. And, if he had anything to do with it, finally rebooking his vacation. Though now the thought of having that sort of time on his hands didn't hold the same allure. It would just give him time to think about Charlotte. Work was a much better idea. Lots and lots of work.

Charlotte woke him later, when dinner service began. He wondered if she was annoyed he'd slept, but she remained as easy and friendly as she had that morning when they'd left the apartment for the last time. "It was good," she'd said, jostling his arm a bit, sighing with satisfaction. "Thank you, Jacob. I'll treasure this time always."

No demands. No tears. Exactly what they'd agreed. He'd hated it.

The chicken tasted like cardboard and even the addition of another whiskey didn't help. He asked for a soft drink afterward, and when he looked over at Charlotte, he saw she'd pulled out her laptop and slid on those ridiculous, sexy little glasses and was working.

For some reason, the sight angered him. His insides were churning from the thought of walking away from her; how could she be so damned calm? Then he noticed that while she was staring at her screen, her fingers weren't moving. She wasn't scrolling, either, to read on farther. She was just…staring.

He was going to miss her. And maybe, just maybe, she was going to miss him, too. It was a bittersweet thought.

But what could he do about it? Nothing.

Nor should he. Instead he decided to watch a movie or something to keep his mind occupied. Otherwise he was going to say something he shouldn't, or touch her or something, and that wouldn't help.

After an hour of staring at his screen and not registering a damned thing, the final approach announcement was made and the crew and passengers started to prepare for landing.

Charlotte closed her laptop and moved to put it in her bag. The scent of her perfume reached him, reminding him of the nights she'd spent wrapped around him, and he didn't want to let her go.

He imagined saying such a thing to her and mentally kicked himself. A woman like Charlotte wouldn't want a man like him, not as a…a partner. She was on her way to even more riches and celebrity and he was a behind-the-scenes guy, still eating beans on toast sometimes. Sure, his business was super successful and in demand. But the way he lived—the way he wanted to live—was so different from her lifestyle.

A quick check out the window showed him they were close to touchdown, and he looked at Charlotte. She was watching him, and a smile touched her lips. "Ready?" she asked.

"First thing I'm going to do is head for a pint at my local," he answered, keeping his voice deliberately light. "Nothing feels more like home. You?"

She shrugged. "To my flat, I guess. I'll see the family tomorrow and be back in the office on Monday. No rest for the wicked."

Her last words sent a jolt of electricity through him. He'd been on the receiving end of her wickedness and it had been heavenly. But he didn't show it. Didn't dare. Goodbye was going to be hard enough. There were so many things to say, but he couldn't, so the result was saying nothing at all of any consequence and feeling awful about it.

The plane touched down and then taxied to the gate. Because they were first class, it was barely a wait at all before they were cleared to leave. Jacob reached into the bin and took out his small case and garment bag—all he'd taken with him for the week. Then he stood back as Charlotte retrieved her smaller bag and smiled at him.

It wobbled just a little.

He had to be the strong one. Nothing good would come of tears or, worse, false promises. They had to leave each other smiling. A clean break and no regrets. He couldn't live with anything else.

Then they were walking toward the gate, the hollow sound of passengers rolling their cases and heavy footsteps filling his ears. Charlotte had to get her bags and go through customs, and Jacob would head in an opposite direction, to go through security to catch his connection. They paused, and Jacob looked down into her sweet, beautiful face. "I guess this is it."

She nodded. "No tears or sappy goodbyes." She smiled and he noticed it didn't wobble this time. "Just thank you. For doing your job, and then for being…" She paused, and his heart constricted. "For being my friend. I'll never forget this week. Not ever."

"Nor will I." His voice came out steady and strong. It had to, no matter what was going on in his head and in his heart. Not since Jacinta had he cared for someone like this. Had he let someone in. Did she realize that? "Take care of yourself, Charlie."

"I will. And you do the same."

And yet neither of them moved. His gaze clung to hers, his hands itched to touch her again. He almost wanted her to ask him to stay. To have one more night with her in Paris before going home to London. But she remained silent, her eyes wide and lips frozen in a smile.

He was leaving. But not without one last kiss.

His bag was over his left shoulder and the garment bag looped over his arm, but he took his right hand and placed it on her cheek, the skin soft beneath his rough palm. He bent his head and touched his lips to hers, gently, as tenderly as a rough soldier like him could manage, needing to taste her and yet ever aware that they were standing in the middle of an airport with crowds milling about them. All too soon he pulled back, but when he did, her eyes were shiny with tears.

"I couldn't go without doing that," he said. What a fool he'd been to agree to her two days of bliss. Now he was addicted. Needed more of her. All of her. And he couldn't have her.

"I'm glad. But you have to go now, Jacob. Saying goodbye isn't one of my talents."

A smile touched his lips. "Mine, either." He adjusted the strap of his bag. "Goodbye, Charlie."

"Goodbye, Jacob."

He turned and walked in the direction of his gate, his heart pounding. Goodbye wasn't enough. But saying "I love you" was too much.

"Home," he murmured, and quickened his stride, refusing to look back.

CHAPTER ELEVEN

Six weeks later

CHARLOTTE STEPPED INSIDE the boardroom and wondered where the hell the coffee was. She was tired all the time. She credited it to putting in long hours since her return from New York, as well as trying to recoup a sleep deficit. Once at home, she'd found it impossible to fall asleep. Her bed seemed too big without Jacob in it. She lay awake night after night, reliving their short time together until exhaustion finally overtook her. For the past few weeks, the insomnia had finally eased. But the fatigue didn't. It was annoying. She didn't have time for this.

No one else had arrived for the meeting yet, so she took advantage of the quiet to take a few deep breaths. It was then she saw the new American *Vogue* issue on a table.

She picked it up and flipped through, looking for Fashion Week coverage. She found it, feeling a persistent sense of anger at the runway shots. Her interview wasn't due to be out until the next issue, and she'd done a followup by phone after the sabotage incident. So it was a surprise when she saw a few photos from the Aurora party included in the coverage. Including one with her smiling and dancing with Jacob, who was smiling one of his rare smiles back down at her.

Mon Dieu, she missed him. More than she wanted to admit.

"That was a spectacular dress choice," her mother said at her shoulder.

Charlotte closed the magazine. "Thank you."

"So many things happened that week. Do you want to finally talk about them?"

Charlotte spun and faced her mother. "What do you mean? We've been through the whole thing with Amelie and how we're going to move forward."

"I don't mean the sabotage, *ma petite*. I mean you. You're different."

Alarm jolted through Charlotte as she tried not to think about what had precipitated that change. Jacob's words, his questioning, his confidence in her. She'd tried to recapture the feeling on her return; updated her wardrobe with some more daring choices and colors, exerted her opinion more readily during meetings. Yet somehow it just wasn't the same. She didn't feel as capable, and couldn't figure out why.

"It's complicated, Maman."

"It usually is when a man is involved."

Charlotte glanced up sharply. "There is no man."

"If you say so."

The coffee service arrived, and Aurora went to fix herself a cup. Charlotte held back. She was so out of sorts today that the smell of the coffee wasn't as inviting as she would have hoped. It actually smelled a bit sharp, acrid. "Is the coffee burnt?"

"I don't think so." Aurora liked hers black and took a sip. "Tastes fine to me. Now, tell me what happened in New York. You gave up your signature look midtrip and then you dealt with Amelie and the canceled show. And then went on to host the party. You did a wonderful job, Charlotte. You really stepped into your own. So why have you been so sad since your return?"

Charlotte's stomach turned at the scent of the coffee, and she reached for one of the peppermint tea bags that were usually meant for Arabella. "I haven't been sad. I've just been tired."

Aurora's brow creased in concern. "You've been working too hard. Getting run-down. Have you had your iron checked?"

"Don't fuss, Maman. I'm fine."

"It has to do with Jacob Wolfe, doesn't it?"

Just hearing his name made her heart ache. How ridiculous. "Jacob Wolfe was my bodyguard. He's a nice man. That's all."

That's all there could be. In six weeks, not once had he tried to make contact. That said it all.

"He's six foot three of gorgeous male that you shared an apartment with for nine days. I would have thought he'd be irresistible."

Charlotte nearly ripped the tea bag in half, taking it out of the paper. "Maman, stop. Please." She dropped the bag in the cup and then added hot water. Mint rose in the steam and she breathed it in. Yes, that was better than coffee.

"Oh, *ma petite*. I am sorry. I was teasing but I can see it is not amusing." She retrieved the magazine and flipped to the page with the picture of them dancing. "You look very happy here. And relaxed. You became…friends?"

Charlotte nodded slightly, a lump in her throat.

"Lovers? Oh, I know, I'm not supposed to ask that of my grown children. But the party was after the sabotage, and he stayed in New York. With you."

"His contract was until the Saturday."

"Sweetheart, I spoke to both of you on that Wednesday. His services were no longer required. He got his fee, but he wasn't under obligation to stay. But he did. Why?"

Holding it inside was killing her. It was silly to think that she'd fallen for someone so quickly, but here she was six weeks later, unable to eat or get enough sleep. She went to a chair and sat down, cradling her cup of tea. Aurora followed and took a chair next to her.

"He stayed because I asked him to. Because he went to the party with me as my friend and that night he became my lover. He made me feel…different. Braver. He let me be myself and wasn't threatened. And he wanted nothing from me. Do you know how rare that is?"

"*Oui, ma petite.*" Aurora put down her cup. "I do." She took Charlotte's hand in hers. "So what went wrong?"

Charlotte pulled away. "Nothing. We have very different lives, and we don't even live in the same country. It would never work."

"Your brother is doing fine with that with Gabi," Aurora pointed out.

"Just because it works for them doesn't mean it would for us. Besides, our jobs keep us both very busy. We don't have time for a relationship."

Aurora sighed. "Well, perhaps it's for the best, then."

Something twigged in Charlotte, got her

hackles up just a bit. Whenever her mother took that "it's for the best" tone, it was never quite sincere. Indeed, it usually ended up with Charlotte feeling flawed and a disappointment.

"What do you mean?" She put down her cup. Maybe the tea wasn't a good idea, either. Her stomach turned over. Or maybe it was conflict making her nauseated.

Aurora crossed her legs and waved a hand in a graceful gesture. "Oh, it's just that if you were really smitten, you wouldn't be finding all kinds of excuses."

Excuses? Charlotte's earlier annoyance turned into a blaze of frustration. "Excuses?" She stood. "You don't think I put in sixty-hour weeks in this job? Or spend my downtime checking emails and doing market research? Do you realize that my entire social life revolves around Aurora Inc. functions? That I never have time to spend with my college friends or…or…"

"What the heck is going on in here?"

Charlotte spun around and saw her twin, William, standing in the door. William, so handsome and happy and perfect. She loved him but right now his perfection was aggravating. Of course he'd nearly thrown everything aside for Gabi, a perfect example of sacrificing for love. Meanwhile, Charlotte was standing there, feeling underappreciated and even a little taken advantage of.

"None of your business." The nausea was overwhelming now. "Please excuse me. I'll be back in a few minutes."

She hurried to the executive bathroom, went inside and locked the door. Maybe a sip of water would help. She ran water and cupped her hand to drink, and the moment she swallowed, the water—and her earlier tea—made a reappearance. Moments later she knelt on the floor, still gasping, tears burning her eyes.

There was only one reason she could think of for being turned off by coffee and throwing up in the bathroom. She hadn't had a period since returning from New York, either.

Ignoring the meeting that was surely now underway, Charlotte took the elevator down to street level and made her way to a pharmacy where she bought a pregnancy test. Then she took it back up to the private bathroom and waited for the results.

It didn't take even the full three minutes. One minute in, the stick told the truth in bright pink. She was pregnant. So much for the withdrawal method working. One time. Just once without protection, and here she was. Bound to be a single mum. Her heart trembled.

How could she expect to do all of this while raising a baby on her own?

After a few minutes of sitting in a stupor, Charlotte got up, touched up her makeup, straightened her skirt and rolled her shoulders. Loads of single mums worked and were fine parents, so why shouldn't she be able to manage? She shook off the fear threatening to still her breath. Charlotte had resources that so many women didn't, so she'd put on her half-English stiff upper lip and get on with it.

The meeting was only forty minutes in and she was supposed to be there. Maybe no one really appreciated how hard she worked, but she'd show them she could do anything. She'd show them all.

Jacob sat at his desk in Richmond and rubbed his hand over his face. Spring had been glorious, and now, deep into April, he should be enjoying the sight of burgeoning gardens and the deep green of the grass on Richmond Green. Instead he'd been in a total funk since arriving back from New York.

It had been hell not to pick up the phone and call Charlotte, or send her a text just to see how she was doing. But what would that achieve? They were not a couple. He knew a total break was best, and he'd get over it eventually.

Like you got over Jacinta?

He frowned.

Jacinta died. It's different.

At least he had nothing to feel guilty about with Charlie. It had been consensual, mutual, and they'd been on exactly the same page about their future.

Keep telling yourself that.

His inner voice just wouldn't shut up.

He opened up a couple of case files and updated them, then moved on to contracts and potential clients. He had two guys in Asia right now, working on a trade mission, and another team in place providing security for a private event in Manchester. Maybe what he really needed was to deploy himself again. Sitting at a desk gave him way too much time to think. Or there was still the issue of his untaken vacation. Either way, he needed to be active again. See if there were any cases he could take on himself.

His mobile vibrated on top of his desk, jumping across the desktop. He grabbed it and answered. "Wolfe Security."

"Jacob?"

He nearly dropped the phone. "Charlie?"

There was a breathless laugh. "It's me."

And then silence, awkward, fell between them. "How are you?" he finally asked, unsure what else to say. Why was she calling him now? It had been two months since they'd said good-bye at the airport.

"I'm—I'm fine." She stuttered a little, but then added, "I'm in London."

Here. She was here.

"For work, I suppose?"

"I was wondering if we could meet for a drink or something."

There was nothing he wanted more than to see her again. Look into her eyes, see her sharp, witty smile. But if he was dragging his ass around like a lost puppy now, wouldn't it be worse if he saw her again?

"I'm not sure that's a good idea."

"Oh. Well. I…uh… I'd really like to see you and talk to you about something."

"You can't run it past me on the phone?"

"I'd prefer not to."

He tapped his fingers on the desk. His self-preservation instinct was quickly being taken over by his overactive curiosity. "Did something happen at Aurora?"

"Let's just meet, okay? I can come to you. You said you have a local pub nearby? Give me the address and I can meet you there, say, around seven?"

She wasn't going to elaborate. Besides, the temptation to see her was too strong to resist.

He gave her the name of the pub and the street it was on and they hung up.

Concentration shot, he got up from his desk and went to the window. The bottom floor of the three-story building served as Wolfe Security offices. There was more than enough square footage for his needs, since he had only three in-house staff and the rest of the employees were generally former military, like him, and on contract. Right now he stared out the window, barely able to make out the park benches on the perimeter of the park. This place was so...civilized. Unlike him. He'd grown up in Lewisham, certainly not a posh life at all. And it wasn't that he didn't enjoy the finer things. He did, in small doses. He knew how to carry himself and never wanted to go back to living paycheck to paycheck, wondering if there'd be enough for a takeaway after bills were paid. On the job, he got to fly to interesting places, eat great food, dress nicely, and all while doing what he was good at. He wasn't complaining.

But there was an expectation that seemed to go along with that kind of living that he didn't warm to. For all the rich had it easy, there was a definite push to "keep up" with each other and maintain a certain standard that he wasn't made for. His bank account might say otherwise, but that wasn't the kind of man he was, deep inside.

He'd told her that back in New York, and nothing had changed.

Which made him even more uneasy about seeing Charlie tonight. What could she possibly want? He wondered if it had something to do with Amelie.

At five, he left his office and went upstairs to the living area of the house. The second floor held a kitchen, living room, study and bathroom. Upstairs were three more bedrooms, two with their own bathrooms. The decor was far more understated than the Pemberton apartment in Manhattan. No big bouquets of flowers or pieces of art. More wood and leather and less light and expensive fabrics. The floors were hardwood, not marble, and old and slightly scarred. This was not in any way a new house. It had been renovated and updated over the decades, but it was solid and didn't try to cover up its history.

It was a lot for him, but the commute was right, since he only had to go downstairs to work and could avoid the tube or city traffic. And it gave him a home base when he wasn't traveling. Now and then, his dad came over to hang out with him and eat greasy fish and chips from paper and drink a few pints.

He took a fresh shower and changed into clean jeans and a pullover, since the evenings were still cool. His hair was due for another cut; he'd had one on his return and usually he required a trim every six weeks. He ran his hands through the blond strands and frowned. Why was he worried so much about what he looked like, what she'd think? They were over.

At ten to seven he was at the door of the pub, hand on the handle, hesitating. Charlie didn't know the depth of his feelings, so all he had to do was keep up the pretense that it had been a special week and a wonderful memory. He just hoped she didn't pull out the "It would be great if we could be friends" line. He wasn't sure he had it in him.

So he squared his shoulders and pulled open the door, and scanned the room for a table.

She was already here. His heart stopped briefly as he caught sight of her, off to the left in a corner, her gaze on the door. Damn, but she was pretty, in a soft-looking sweater and her sleek hair tucked behind one ear. And her smile… She was smiling at him, a big, welcoming, I'm-glad-to-see-you smile that hit him right in the gut as he smiled back because truthfully, it was good to see her. More than good. Like all the weight of the last two months lifted off his shoulders somehow. Alarm bells started ringing in his head.

He went to her and she got up, and he kissed

her cheek, trying to be welcoming and also platonic and failing miserably because the scent of her turned him into a marshmallow. "Charlie. It's good to see you."

Nice, warm, pleasant. But not too much. He congratulated himself, considering the way his pulse was hammering.

"It's good to see you, too, Jacob."

"Have you eaten? The food's good here."

"I did, yes. But you can order if you'd like."

He didn't want to be the only one eating, so he shook his head. "I'm fine. I'll get a pint, though. What can I get you?"

"Just a tonic water, slice of lime."

He grinned. "No gin?"

"Not tonight." Her smile was in place but there was something behind it that was intriguing. She wasn't as comfortable as she tried to appear, and he wondered why. Was his local pub a little too "local" for her tastes? He ordered their drinks and then turned back to her.

"What brings you to the city?"

Charlotte paused, and then looked him in the eyes. "Truthfully, you."

"Me?" He frowned. "Did something happen with Amelie? Do you need me to give a statement or anything?"

She shook her head. "No, the thing with Amelie's pretty much resolved. She's left Paris with Marie for a new start. How they do that doesn't matter to me, as long as they keep Aurora out of it."

Their drinks arrived and she poked at the lime wedge with her little straw. "The truth is, Jacob, I came here to tell you something in person that I didn't want to tell you over the phone."

His pulse took on a different drumming now, not one of anticipation but a slow thudding that told him something big was coming. She'd found someone else. She was getting married. Though why she'd have to tell him that in person was beyond him...

"Whatever it is, I promise I'm fine, Charlie. Just tell me." He lifted his glass for a sip.

"I'm pregnant."

He nearly spit out the beer; instead he inhaled and started to cough. Had she said...pregnant? He put down his glass and stared at her, his lips dropped open. "You're...but we..." Realization hit him and he closed his eyes. "Except that first time. Even though we were careful."

"Yes," she said softly, so that he barely heard her over the voices and the music in the background. "Except that first time."

And now she was having his baby.

"You're sure? You've taken a test, seen a doctor?"

She nodded. "Yes, to both questions. I'm two

months along now. And Jacob? There was no one else. Not before, and not since."

He hadn't even been going to ask her that. "Of course," he said, letting out a massive breath. "I would never think you'd lie, Charlie. Your conscience would eat you alive."

She smiled then. "Thank you. For believing me."

Jacob ran his hand over his face, then took a rather bracing swig of beer. It said a lot about the people she'd been involved with that she'd have to thank him for accepting she was telling the truth. When he put his glass down again, he felt ready to say what he needed to say. "Whatever you want or need from me, you've got it."

She sat back and lifted her highball glass, almost as if she was hiding behind it. What was she going to ask him for? Money? She had plenty of that, though he would gladly support his kid financially. The air strangled in his throat. Marriage? Or the opposite—signing away any parental rights? Any of those options made him feel faint, something that a man in his line of work never felt. He was going to be a father. His head swam with the words. He'd stared down the barrel of a gun more times than he could count. Nothing had weakened him like impending fatherhood.

"I don't know what I want," she finally said,

looking down at the table. "It took me by surprise a few weeks ago." She looked up and her gaze touched his and then slid away. "I'm financially set, and my family is wonderful. I can do this on my own if I want to."

So why did she sound so unsure beneath the bravado?

"I'm sure you can."

"I'm not after anything. We agreed to two days together, then we said goodbye. No ties. No lingering emotions. Just good memories."

His fingers tightened around the glass. "This is much bigger than a memory."

Charlotte's eyes narrowed. "Then what do you want? Certainly not to be a father. And I know you're not interested in a relationship."

"How do you know that?"

She stilled, stared at him. "What do you mean?"

"How do you know I'm not interested in a relationship?"

"Because of Jacinta."

She said the name so bluntly that he winced. But since New York he'd had time to think, too much time. There were things he wanted to say that he couldn't say here, in a busy pub on a weeknight.

"I live two streets over," he said, then drained the last of his pint. "Why don't you come over, have something to eat, and we can talk about this."

"I got a hotel."

"I'm sure. And I'm not asking you to stay the night, though you're more than welcome. I have lots of space." He leaned across the table. "This is an important conversation, Charlie. I'd rather have it in private."

She nodded, her face paler than he remembered it, and reached for her handbag. He tossed some notes on the table to cover their drinks and a tip and then escorted her outside into the spring air.

She inhaled deeply and let it out. "Oh, the fresh air is nice."

He glanced at her profile, and the wan tone of her skin. "Have you been sick?" Jacob knew next to nothing about pregnancy and babies, but everyone knew about morning sickness. And that it didn't just happen in the morning.

She nodded. "A little, not too much. Smells, more than anything, seem to set me off. The food in there was fine. The smell of the beer, though…was a little rough."

"Sorry." If he'd known he would have ordered differently.

"No, it's okay. The tonic was perfect. Fizzy water with lime is my current go-to."

"I'm just a few blocks. This way." He started

down the pavement and she kept step with him, her flats slapping lightly on the surface.

"No heels?"

"Not tonight." She'd dressed down in jeans and the sweater and looked very cuddleable. "I've been saving them for the office. You'll also be surprised to hear that I'm off coffee. The smell turns my stomach. I've started drinking my sister's herbal teas."

"You? Without caffeine?"

That coaxed a smile out of her. "I know. That's how I knew. I smelled coffee and made a dash for the bathroom."

His head was still swimming with the fact that she was pregnant and he was going to be a father. He had no business having a kid. He wasn't the kind to settle down. While the danger was lessened, he still put himself in the line of fire in his job. He and his dad had muddled through as best they could, but he wanted more for his kid. Not just muddling through, but he had no idea how to do that. Especially how to do that when he lived in London and Charlie was in Paris.

Moreover, what did he have to offer that the Pembertons couldn't provide? Never before had the gap in their lives seemed so large.

Their steps grew slower as they turned onto his street. "Richmond is lovely, isn't it?" Charlotte said. "Look there, that little house with the cute door and the little garden. It's like something out of a storybook."

"I like it here. I started out by renting the ground floor for my business, and then ended up buying the building. It didn't make sense for me to pay for two places when I could make my home upstairs. It's a bit bigger than this place, though."

When they finally stopped in front of his building, her eyes widened. "Oh. It is big. Larger than I expected."

"The entire business is run from the ground floor. I have three employees plus me on staff, and everyone else works remotely, including my tech team. I live on the top two floors." He turned to her. "Private security is lucrative, Charlie. I know you'll say you don't need it, but I can support my child."

He unlocked the door and guided her through to the stairs that led to the second floor. As her steps echoed behind him, he had a sudden, jarring thought. She'd said she could do it on her own *if she wanted to.*

Did that mean she was considering not having the baby?

A war went on within his heart. He'd always supported a woman's right to choose, and this was certainly unplanned. At the same time, supporting her would come at a personal cost. A lump grew in his throat. He hadn't planned to be a father, but life didn't go to plan hardly ever. He would support her either way, even if it hurt.

"Are you all right?"

He'd been standing in front of the upstairs door for several seconds, but hadn't opened it. He turned the knob and went inside, flicking on a light. "I'm fine. Just got into my head for a moment there." He turned to face her. "Charlie, I have to ask you. Are you considering terminating this pregnancy?"

CHAPTER TWELVE

CHARLOTTE STARED AT HIM, stunned by his question. Had she given him that impression? If she had, it wasn't deliberate. But she was very glad he'd asked her here and not in the pub.

"Can we sit down or something, please?" She'd said she was fine in the pub, but truthfully she hadn't eaten any dinner and wasn't feeling super great. Even the tonic water hadn't settled her stomach. She was hungry, plain and simple.

"Of course." He led her to a leather sofa and she sank down into the rich cushions. She looked around as he took a seat in the chair next to the sofa. This place suited him, and she liked it quite a bit. Rich wood and leathers, but lots of windows, which she guessed overlooked Richmond Green though she couldn't tell now, in the deep of twilight. It was masculine but it was also ridiculously cozy. The kind of room where you could curl up with a book and a glass of wine and let the worries of the world fade away.

Maybe, because of his profession, that was just what he needed.

She clasped her hands and looked up at him. He was waiting for her to respond, but not pressuring. She answered him as plainly as possible. "I'm not now. I did consider it as one of my options, but I've decided to keep the baby." His expression was inscrutable. "Would it have been a problem if I had?"

He held her gaze. "I would have supported you either way. But I'm not going to lie. I find myself relieved."

She appreciated his honesty. And was glad to know he had feelings about it. She certainly had gone back and forth for a while. It had been hard telling the family, too. Charlotte was often the perfect by-the-book child. She was the one who didn't make ripples or waves. A baby in the family was a big ripple.

And this was the first grandchild. A grandchild her father would never meet. She felt the pain of that every day.

"Charlotte, what do you want from me? Why are you here?"

It was so hard sitting across from him. All she could think about was their time together and how safe and secure she'd felt. How she'd relaxed when relax wasn't really something she ever did. "I told you. I thought this was the kind of news to deliver in person."

"Fair." He leaned ahead, resting his elbows on his knees. "But you must have some idea about what you think this should look like." He motioned with his finger, going back and forth between them. "You always have a plan, Charlie. So what's the plan?"

They'd known each other for nine days and he already knew that about her. "I'll raise the baby on my own. I can have a career and a child. I'll have lots of help and I have it so much better than most women. Financial security is not an issue for me. I'm very lucky, really."

Then she smiled, and meant it. She knew how fortunate she was. "My sister, Arabella, is already making sounds about being an auntie and Maman is making plans for a nursery at the chateau. I have lots of support."

He leaned back. "Then what you're saying is you don't need me."

She hadn't meant it that way, and knew she had to tread carefully now. "Jacob, you need to take time to think about this. I would never deny you access to see your child. That's not right. But if you don't want to be a part of this, I want to know before the baby is born. The last thing I want is for my child to have a father who passes in and out of their life, setting up expectations and delivering disappointments. If you don't want this, it's okay. But if you do want to be a part, we need to talk down the road about what that will look like."

His gray eyes flared and she knew she'd hit a nerve. His eyes were the same flinty color as when he'd been angry with her in New York. It was okay, though. She hadn't expected this to be an easy conversation.

"You expect me to just walk away and pretend my child doesn't exist?" He let out a huff. "I know we were only together a short time, but I thought you knew me better than that. I have a duty and I don't intend to shirk it."

Her heart stumbled. She didn't want his parenthood to be a "duty." "Please, don't do this out of some sense of obligation. I'd rather you not be involved at all than consider visitation some sort of obligation to check off on the calendar."

He got up from the chair and began to pace. She'd upset him again, but these were things that needed to be said. He ran his hand through his hair—he needed a cut, she noticed, and the urge to sink her fingers into the soft strands was overwhelming. They were talking parenting logistics here, so why was she thinking about touching him? Not helpful at all.

Jacob finally faced her. "I think you and I have differing definitions of duty," he said.

"It's not the same as an obligation, which to me has a very different connotation. Duty…that is something I choose. I do it consciously, fully recognizing the implications of it. I joined the military of my own free will, and then I had a duty…to my country, to my unit, to my team. It came with risks and rewards, but it was something I chose to bind myself to. When I left the Forces and started this business, I chose duty again. Duty to my clients, of course, but duty to my team to make sure they have the best information and resources possible.

"This baby didn't ask to be conceived. And I could walk away, I suppose. But that's not the type of man I am. And so my duty doesn't come from an obligation but from a place deep inside me. A willing place, a place where I choose to do what's right. That sort of duty isn't a burden. It's an honor."

She blinked back tears. He was such a good man. But he didn't love her. And she wasn't sure she loved him… How could she after such a brief fling?

Besides, nothing had changed. He still ran his company from here and she lived and worked in Paris. He certainly prospered but did so without the intrusive celebrity that came with being a Pemberton. He'd made it into a magazine but he'd never been hit with the tabloids. Being part of the Pemberton family was a whole other level of everything. While many yearned to be a part of that world, it wasn't Jacob's style. He'd be miserable, wouldn't he?

"Okay," she whispered, still emotional after his speech. "Okay, then, we'll figure it out. You'll be a part of our baby's life." And a part of hers, she realized. She'd be tied to him forever. It sent a pain rippling through her chest. Tied to him without having him. Maybe it would get easier with time.

He sat beside her on the sofa. "Do you need anything? It must sound ridiculous, I suppose. If you needed something, you could just buy it."

"What I needed was to tell you, to see where your head's at." She wet her lips, which were suddenly dry. "You didn't disappoint me. You never have."

"I try," he replied, and nudged her shoulder with his own.

She laughed a little, and the sound trailed away, a bit wistfully, she realized.

"Are you scared?" he asked.

The question came as such a relief that she bobbed her head up and down quickly. "Oh, thank God you asked that. No one has. I'm terrified."

"Come here." He lifted his arm and made room for her to curl in next to his shoulder.

She knew she shouldn't but couldn't resist. He was so solid and warm, reassuring. She closed her eyes as his arm circled around her and kept her close.

"It had to be a shock. Hell, I'm still shocked. We shouldn't have been so careless."

Charlotte didn't know what to say. To admit that the fire between them had burned too hot to stop would add an element of *something* to this evening she wasn't ready to discuss. "Well, it's done. We're going to be parents. I figure we'll just do a lot of learning as we go." She craned her neck to look up at him. "If we can act as if we're on the same team, I think it'll be okay."

"Act? We are on the same team. We want the same things, right? Listen, I lost my mom young and it was just me and my dad. We did okay, but I want more for my kid. I'll be there for them whenever I can."

"And your dad now? Are you two still close?"

He nodded. "I don't see him as much as I'd like, but yeah, we're close. We get together for some drinks and darts at the pub 'round the corner from where I grew up. He's still with the Met, but on a desk now."

"I'm glad. That you still have each other."

"Me, too."

"So our baby will have a grandfather after all," she said, the thought warming her.

"And a doting one, I wager." Her stomach chose that moment to rumble. He chuckled and looked down at her. "Hungry?"

"I lied at the pub. I didn't eat."

"Hmm. Let me fix something."

"You don't have to. I can go back to the hotel and order room service—"

"And it won't arrive until nearly ten o'clock. I can cook, remember? What are your no-go foods?"

She laughed. "Coffee, tomatoes, runny eggs." She shuddered. "For some reason, I cannot do yolks right now."

"Don't worry. I've got this. You relax and I won't be long."

He shifted out from under her and headed for the kitchen, while she leaned back against the sofa cushions and marveled at the life events that had brought her to this moment, in his house. She looked around, taking in the fine draperies, the huge rug in the middle of the floor, the expensive lamps. It reminded her a little of the room at Chatsworth Manor that the family used for their casual use, rather than the more formal drawing room. She got up from the sofa and made her way to the kitchen, where Jacob had his head stuck in the stainless steel fridge.

"Do you mind if I give myself a tour?"

"Not at all." He straightened and smiled.

"This floor has the kitchen, dining room, small bath and a study. Upstairs are the bedrooms and other bathrooms." His gaze touched hers. "I did mean it about you staying if you want. I do have room."

But not in his room. And she wasn't sure she could stand being down the hall from him again, imagining him in bed, his chest bare, his long legs with one sticking outside the covers.

She didn't respond, but instead backed away and went to explore.

The half bath was lovely, with a small marble counter and gold taps. She'd noticed the kitchen had a nook for eating, and the dining room was rather splendid, with a table that seated eight and a sideboard that she was absolutely envious of. But it was the study that drew her in and made her catch her breath. So much dark wood, from the woodwork to the gleaming floors to the massive bookshelves that covered the walls. And the shelves were full of books. New ones, old ones, spines faded and worn. There was a magnificent rolltop desk and chair, and a fireplace with comfortable chairs around it. For a moment she imagined sitting in one of these chairs, a fire blazing, reading a bedtime story to their child.

But that wouldn't happen, would it? If anyone read bedtime stories here, it would be Jacob.

There would be times their child would visit here, without her, spending time with Jacob, while she would be home, missing both of them.

She wrapped an arm around herself, suddenly lonely.

The upstairs was equally gorgeous. Each bedroom had its own four-poster bed, with rich linens and matching window coverings. The bathrooms were stunning, with huge soaker tubs and separate showers. Buying this place had to cost a fortune. Renovating it cost even more. Jacob wasn't lying when he said his business provided well. Yet you would never know he was wealthy in his own right. There were no airs put on. He was just an ordinary guy.

There was something refreshing about that.

When she arrived back downstairs, she found him in the kitchen, putting sandwiches on plates. "Nothing fancy," he said, smiling. "Cheese toasties."

"That's perfect." There was something so comforting about a simple cheese sandwich. He'd poured her a glass of water, too, and put everything at the small table in the kitchen's eating nook.

"If you like we can move this to the dining room."

She caught his eye and saw he was teasing. "This is fine." She took a bite and tasted butter and cheese and sighed in appreciation. "This is just what I needed. Thank you, Jacob."

"You're welcome."

They munched for a few minutes in silence, until the quiet became uncomfortable. "So... How's business been since you've been back?"

Jacob wiped his hands on a napkin. "Good. I've been in the office the whole time, though. I was just thinking today I might like to take another assignment. I can only stand being behind a desk for so long."

She nodded, but the bite of sandwich seemed stuck in her mouth. Another assignment. He did have wandering feet, didn't he?

"I didn't realize you did assignments anymore. I thought mine was to cover for someone who'd been sick."

"It was. I wasn't scheduled to take your job because I was supposed to be on vacation. But I do put myself on the rotation. It keeps me sharp."

And in danger, she thought. Guarding her hadn't been that dangerous. It had been an employee with a gripe, who'd wanted to hit back at Aurora Inc. but not harm her physically. That wasn't always the case, though, was it? I mean, who hired bodyguards if there wasn't a threat?

"What's wrong?" he asked, and she shook her head and reached for her sandwich again.

"Nothing. I guess I just never thought of you

being, what do you call it, in the field? On a regular basis."

He finished his sandwich and rose, taking his plate to the dishwasher. "I'm thirty-seven, Charlie. Not ready to be shut up in an office all day yet. Not sure if I ever will."

"Does anyone ever get hurt on the job?"

He shut the dishwasher door and turned to face her. "Our job is to keep people safe. Including us."

"But still, the potential is there."

"Well, I could step outside tomorrow and get hit by a bus."

She'd heard that kind of logic before, but it didn't make sense. That was an accident. That wasn't deliberately putting oneself in harm's way. He was going to be her baby's father. What if something happened to him? She'd had her father until her midtwenties, and even then, losing him had been horrible. But she couldn't imagine growing up without his presence. With that gaping hole in her life at such a crucial time. She'd lost her father. The idea of losing the father to her child was devastating—whether or not they were together.

It was turning out that the very thing that had brought them together—his vocation—was the thing that scared her most about their future as co-parents.

She pushed away the rest of the sandwich. Not just co-parents, not that she'd say that out loud to him. She cared for him so much. Still remembered how it felt to be held in his arms in the dark. The way he kissed her as if she was the most cherished thing in the world. She couldn't bear thinking of a world without him in it.

He came back to the table and pulled out a chair, then sat close to her. "Look," he said softly, putting his hand on her leg. "I'm always careful. I'm going to be around for a long time. Trust me."

But trust wasn't something that came easy to her. Not after years of either being left or being used. And it was impossible to trust something that was largely out of his control.

Nothing had changed—their lives were too different. She had to find a way to resolve her feelings, didn't she? Let go of any romantic notions and, like she said earlier, be a team.

"I'm tired. I think I should head back to my hotel."

"Are you sure you don't want to stay here? I've got lots of room."

Staying under the same roof tonight wouldn't be good. She'd get ideas and feelings and she wasn't sure how good her willpower was where he was involved. "I think the hotel is best. But I'm glad we talked."

"Me, too. I still need to wrap my head around the news, but I'd like to meet again before you return to Paris."

"I'd planned to stay a few more days and then weekend at the manor house." The thought of floating around the huge house for three days made her lonesome. "Why don't you come with me? There's tons of privacy there. It'll give you a few days to think about things and then maybe we can make some sort of plan."

The more she thought about it, the more the idea had merit. It was unrealistic to think that they'd come up with any sort of resolution in a few hours, when he'd barely had time to absorb the news. She'd had a few weeks now to get her footing.

"Chatsworth Manor, you mean."

"I do. It's beautiful right now, with everything newly green and blooming. Do you ride? We could go 'round the grounds—"

"One, no I don't ride. And two, are you sure you should, being pregnant?"

She refused to let him bring down her mood. She needed…to go home. That was the manor house to her. The place she'd done most of her growing up, where most of her memories were. The chateau was for holidays and summer, but the manor… That was where she felt most safe and secure, things she needed in her life right now.

"Walks in the garden, then. I think we need this, Jacob. To sort through it all."

He paused, watching her for a long time. She wished she was better at reading his mind, but expected shuttering away was a talent he'd perfected years ago. Finally he agreed. "All right. I'll go. Let me know where to pick you up and we can drive down together."

"I'll text you everything." She got up from the table and went to him. "I'm sorry, you know. This isn't what either of us planned. But we'll deal with it okay, right?"

"Of course we will."

She called a taxi and then he walked her downstairs and outside, into the cool spring night. In less than a minute, the black cab rolled up to the curb.

"You'll text?"

She nodded, suddenly not wanting to say goodbye, knowing she had to. She kept thinking about how he said he stayed on rotation with the company, to keep "sharp." And while she cared about him, he hadn't made any move to kiss her or remotely suggest that there be a romantic element to this situation. In that, nothing had changed. He didn't want a relationship, and his work, filled with travel and what he'd call "calculated risk," wasn't exactly conducive to hands-on parenting, was it?

"I'll be in touch. Take some time to think and we'll see if we can come up with an arrangement on the weekend."

"Take care," he said softly, and opened the door to the cab.

She slid inside and he closed the door. Once she gave the address to the driver, she sat back against the seat and fought tears.

Nothing seemed right. Nothing at all.

CHAPTER THIRTEEN

Jacob stared up at the manor house and wondered what the heck he'd got himself into.

He grabbed his duffel from the back of the Land Rover and also Charlotte's bag. She was hopping out of the passenger side of the vehicle and he swallowed thickly. He'd sat beside her for the better part of two hours as they made their way through London and then down to the estate, going through the picturesque village of Bramley on their way. It had been its own special sort of torture. His gaze kept sliding to his left, to her still-flat stomach. His baby was in there. A human being they'd created together. He'd made a career of dealing with difficult situations, but this one nearly bowled him over.

"You coming?" she called, starting to walk toward the front doors. "I'm hungry and I'm sure Mrs. Flanagan has everything ready for us."

He picked up the pace to catch up with her,

carrying the bags along the narrow cobblestone walk flanked by very precisely trimmed shrubs. "Mrs. Flanagan?"

"The housekeeper." Charlotte's smile was wide as she looked over her shoulder. "She's a wonder. Been the housekeeper here for as long as I can remember. Pretty sure she was hired before I was born."

A housekeeper. "I suppose there's a cook, as well?"

She laughed. "Yes, and a couple of maids. We don't live here full-time but we use it enough that staff is here year-round. Stephen is here often, and Christmas is always here. You should see the house at the holidays. It's gorgeous."

He had no doubt. It was already glorious, with extensive gardens. "How old is this place, anyway?"

She stopped at the steps leading to the doors. "It was built in the seventeenth century. My great-great-grandfather, Edward Pemberton, bought it and it became the country home for the Earl of Chatsworth. And so it was my father's home and now it is Stephen's."

Jacob wasn't afraid of money or fame. In his line of work, he came into contact with a lot of both. But it was different, knowing he was fathering a child into such a family. Being a bodyguard was a totally different dynamic than being a dad. Not much threw him off balance, but this did. If he'd been out of place in New York, being at the country home of the Pemberton family was like another universe.

And then the doors opened and he stepped into Chatsworth Manor.

"Miss Charlotte! Oh, it's good to see you back." A middle-aged woman, her red hair streaked with a little gray, came forward and gave Charlotte a hug. "How are you feeling? Do you need anything special while you're here?"

"Maman told you," Charlotte said dryly.

"Of course she did. You let us know if there are any foods that don't agree with you right now, or anything you need at all." Her eyes shone. "I'm delighted there's going to be a baby in the house. And that's all I'll say about that."

Charlotte gave the housekeeper another squeeze. "Oh, I doubt that's all. Mrs. Flanagan, this is Jacob Wolfe. Jacob, our housekeeper, Mrs. Flanagan."

"Pleased to meet you," he said, and nodded.

"You're the one?"

He was surprised at being put on the spot and by the housekeeper no less, but he met her gaze and answered, "Yes, ma'am."

Mrs. Flanagan's eyes were sharp. "Then you'd better treat Miss Charlotte right. And that's all I'll say about that."

He was starting to think that was her go-to phrase, and that it meant exactly the opposite, and despite himself he was charmed.

"Charlotte deserves all the good things," he agreed, and smiled.

She lifted an eyebrow. "Miss Charlotte, you brought home a charmer."

Charlotte laughed then, and he realized how much he'd missed the sound. There'd been no laughing the other night when they'd spoken, but hearing it now filled him with...well, happiness.

Be careful, his heart said. The last time he'd felt this kind of unfettered joy it had been ripped away so cruelly.

"I'm going to get settled in my room," Charlotte said. "Mrs. Flanagan, where should I put Jacob?"

"We've readied the blue room down from yours."

"Thank you, Mrs. Flanagan. We'll be down for dinner at seven."

"Very good."

Charlotte turned away and Mrs. Flanagan's voice stopped her again. "Charlotte?"

Jacob watched as Charlotte turned back.

"It's very good to have you home, love."

"It's good to be home," she replied softly, and then she led Jacob up the stairs.

He followed, still carrying the bags, and before too long they were at Charlotte's bedroom door. He deposited her suitcase inside, and stared at her bed. It was the most original, beautiful piece of ironwork he'd ever seen and must weight a ton. A four-poster, but each post had iron twisted around it like vines, with leaves, flowers and more vines creating a canopy over top. The walls were a soft sage green with white trim, and the bedding and draperies had a softer sage green background with delicate pink and yellow blossoms. It was like walking into a garden.

"Wow," he said, stepping farther into the room. "I thought the rooms at the Manhattan apartment were gorgeous, but this... This is amazing."

"Maman and Father let me decorate it myself when I was sixteen. I chose the furniture and fabrics myself, and I've never had the heart to change it."

"Remind me why you're in PR and not design or something?"

To his surprise, she blushed. "I do help William out on the fashion side of things. It's why I was so happy to go to New York for Fashion Week. The thing is, we, as family members, don't really do much of the designing or formulating. We run the business. Of course we love it all, so the disconnect is one of function only."

"You certainly seem to have a talent, though." He still couldn't get over how stunning her room was. "Have you thought about doing a home design part of the business?"

She laughed. "You're good for my ego, Jacob. And truthfully, not home design. I have a secret thing for shoes, and it's one of the few things Aurora hasn't delved into yet."

"Then you should." He put his hand on her shoulder. "You should do whatever sets you on fire, Charlie."

Shock gripped him as she spun around and pressed her lips to his. He opened to her fully; he'd wanted to do this each day since they'd last seen each other. She tasted like spring and the mint tea from their drive, and he dropped his duffel and put his arms around her, pulling her close.

Thank God. He'd started to think that she was over what had happened in New York.

She ended the kiss and stepped back, pressing her fingers to her lips. "Oops," she said softly.

"That didn't feel accidental to me," he replied, and he looked at her lips again, biting down on his own. Hers were plump and pink, waiting to be kissed again.

"Not accidental…maybe impulsive?" She giggled a bit, as if she were nervous. "You said to do what sets me on fire…"

"Be careful," he warned. "That's what got us here in the first place."

Her face changed, sobering. "God, you're right. I'm sorry."

"Don't apologize. We're here to talk about what we want for the future. This has to be part of that discussion, don't you think? We shouldn't dance around it. It'll only complicate things."

"I agree." She lifted her chin. "We're here to set out terms, not for some weekend getaway." She gestured toward the door with her hand. "Shall we? I'll show you to your room. You can get settled and we can meet for dinner."

Charlotte was resetting the baseline for their conversation and he understood and appreciated it. Still, he was glad she'd kissed him, with such passion and longing. It gave him hope. They had nearly seven months before the baby was born. Time in which he could show her how he felt about her. Time for her to maybe fall in love with him the way he'd fallen in love with her.

Because in the days since she'd told him the news, he'd been able to come to only one conclusion. He wanted to be with her, even if it was messy. Even if he was intimidated and out of place. Life was just better with her in it. He found himself wanting things he hadn't wanted for years. Money be damned, status be damned... He wanted to be a father to this baby and he wanted to love its mother the best way he knew how. The way his father had loved his mother until she died. And the way Cedric Pemberton had loved Aurora.

Coming home had been the right choice.

Charlotte stepped outside into the back garden and breathed deeply. This time of year, the gardens were really coming into their own. The wisteria wound along a pergola and draped its fragrant blossoms in massive clumps of light purple. The roses weren't quite on, but the buds were plump and near to blooming. The azaleas were bright pink and gorgeous, and her personal favorite, lilac, filled the air with the sweet scent she equated to love and security.

She loved the chateau. She loved her flat in Paris. But Chatsworth Manor would always be home to her. She wished her father were here now, to offer his guidance and wisdom. She reached out to the profusion of clematis leaves and flowers, her fingertips touching the trellis that supported the vines. Cedric Pemberton would not have been overjoyed at her being pregnant without the benefit of marriage, or at least in a long-term relationship rather than a weeklong fling. But he would have put that aside to support her, to help her sort the threads of confusion into a solid plan for the future. He'd always been a grounding force, and she'd never missed him so much.

That Jacob reminded her of her dad didn't help, either. He had the same steadiness, the same calm in the face of the storm. Unfortunately, he was also part of the problem. Every time she considered seeing if something could work between them, she remembered the scars on his body, evidence that in years past he'd been a target. Knife wounds and gunshot wounds... And still he chose to put himself in front of people for their protection. She could admire it and still not be willing to take that on herself, couldn't she?

And then there was still the question of Jacinta. Charlotte knew Jacob had loved her utterly. There was no denying that. She cared for Jacob, but she refused to be with someone, in a real relationship, when that person was still in love with someone else. Even if that someone else was a ghost.

Which kept circling her back to the same issue: how to manage her feelings for Jacob and come up with a workable plan so their child would grow up knowing both parents.

The walk in the gardens had helped calm her

mind, so she went inside and got ready for dinner. It would be just the two of them tonight, and Charlotte knew Mrs. Flanagan would have told the cook to have some of Charlotte's favorites during the weekend. Her mouth watered just thinking about it. Charlotte had learned to cook, but her skills were rudimentary at best. Oh, it was good to be home.

She found Jacob in the dining room, looking up at one of the paintings with a thoughtful expression. "You're early," she said.

"Occupational hazard," he replied, dragging his gaze away from the art and settling it on her. "I go in and assess ahead of time. On time for me is fifteen minutes early."

She smiled. "And yet I was at the pub before you the other night."

"So you were. But then I discovered you are generally very prompt."

"I was nervous. I wanted to control the situation."

He went to her then. He hadn't changed. He still wore jeans and a light sweater, and she was glad they hadn't dressed for dinner. There was no point, was there? It was just the two of them, after all.

"You don't have to be nervous with me." He reached out and took her hand. "I don't want to make this more difficult for you, Charlie. I want us to work as a team."

She pulled her hand away. Ugh, a team. Like the guys he worked with, she supposed. Approach this in a tactical way as if her heart wasn't involved. She knew he was right but resented that it seemed to be so easy for him.

Dinner was served then, and Charlotte smiled fondly as she looked down at her plate. One of her favorites—steak and Guinness pie, with a side of garlic mash and French green beans.

"This smells amazing," Jacob said, picking up his fork. "I'll confess I'm a little surprised. It's very, uh…"

"Ordinary? Did you expect something you couldn't recognize or pronounce? I promise, the Pembertons can be quite normal." She lifted her fork with a piece of savory beef and put it in her mouth. The rich flavor exploded on her tongue. "We have a great cook and this was one of my favorites growing up. It's lovely that she still remembers."

"Your staff has been with you a long time," he observed, digging into his meal.

"Many of them for years. I know it's going to sound strange saying they're like family, but it really isn't like all that upstairs/downstairs nonsense from TV. Yes, we pay them a wage, but you get to know people. Mrs. Flanagan, for instance. She was widowed a few years back, has a lovely daughter named Esme who is around my age. Mrs. Flanagan never drove, but when her husband died, she finally went to get her license. When she decided to get a newer car, my dad went with her on the test drive and ensured she could get financing."

The memory made her smile. The two of them had taken the older car in to trade and Mrs. Flanagan had driven the new car, a cute little hatchback, right up the main drive with the Earl sitting in the passenger seat grinning broadly.

"You miss your father."

She swallowed around the sudden lump in her throat. "Terribly," she admitted. "But we're all managing okay, aren't we?" Determined, she continued with her meal. "Now, we should discuss the baby. Did you come up with any ideas during our days apart?"

He took a long drink of iced water and then put the glass back down. "Nothing concrete. I think a good starting place, though, is for me to tell you that I want to make this work. I want to be there for you and for our child. I don't ever want my kid to feel they don't have a father, or that I'm not invested in their happiness." He looked at her evenly. "And that means making sure our relationship is solid, based on respect and consideration. Whatever this ends up looking like, those are my non-negotiables."

"Mine, too." She let out a sigh of relief. "I think what I want from you isn't material, Jacob. Clearly, I'm set financially. This is more about... well, our child's sense of security and family."

"I know. What does that look like for you?" He watched her with an expectant expression, and for some reason she felt a strange pressure to say the right thing.

What it looked like in her heart wasn't what logic dictated. In her heart she saw the two of them, making coffee like they did in the morning in New York, maybe Jacob still in his workout clothes. Saw a little boy or girl come into the kitchen, looking for breakfast from Mum or Dad. That was where the logic jumped in and self-corrected. After breakfast Dad would take his duffel with him when he left for two weeks or a month, putting himself between his client and the threat.

She wasn't really hungry anymore.

"What's wrong? Are you still nauseated?" Jacob's face tightened with concern and he got up from his chair, going to her side. And at that precise moment, the dining room door opened and Stephen strode in.

Charlotte collected herself quickly. "Stephen! We didn't expect you."

"Nor did I." His face looked appropriately contrite. "What I mean is… I didn't know you'd be here. With company." His gaze moved to Jacob.

Jacob rose and held out his hand. "Jacob Wolfe."

Stephen shook it firmly. "Stephen Pemberton. Earl of Chatsworth and Charlotte's big brother."

They dropped hands and to her surprise Jacob smiled at Stephen's obvious staking of territory. "Of course. Shall I address you as My Lord?"

"Only if you hurt my sister."

Jacob's grin widened. "Join us for dinner, won't you?"

Through all this Charlotte had remained silent, but now she spoke up. "Actually, Stephen, Jacob and I were having a private conversation."

"Which we can continue later, can't we?" Jacob looked down at her. "It's okay, Charlie. We have time. It's all going to work out fine. We want the same things."

Oh, she doubted it, but she understood what he meant. Stephen took the seat opposite Jacob and flipped his napkin open before putting it on his lap. Another meal appeared for Stephen, who sighed with appreciation.

"I've missed the food here," he admitted.

Charlotte nodded. "It's good. Why are you

here, Stephen? I didn't recall seeing anything on the family chat."

"I've got to be in London next week, and thought a weekend here would be a nice break. We don't come here as much since…"

He stopped, but she knew the end of the sentence. Since Dad died.

"Anyway," he carried on, "I didn't realize you'd be here or I would have given you your privacy." He looked at Jacob. "You are the father, yes?"

Jacob's gaze was even and unflappable. "Yes."

"We should meet for a drink later this evening."

"Stephen, I really don't think—"

"Of course. I'd like that."

She cleared her throat. "As long as you stay away from the antique dueling pistols. Stephen, I can handle myself."

He put on an innocent face. "Of course you can."

She leaned closer to him. "And your interference with Will and Gabi was not appreciated. Hint-hint."

He raised an eyebrow. "Entirely different situation." He looked back at Jacob. "I'm sure you can understand, that since our father is no longer here…"

"I understand completely. If I had a sister, I'd feel exactly the same."

"Good." Satisfied, Stephen tucked into his meal as if he hadn't eaten all day, and to her surprise, so did Jacob. It was like they'd spoken some secret male language and come away with a satisfactory conclusion. Puzzling. And she didn't like it, either. She called her own shots. Still, Stephen had been through a lot the last several months. Probably better to let him flex his big-brother muscles and then talk to Jacob again once it was over.

Dessert was another of her favorites, treacle tart, which Jacob exclaimed over and then sat back and patted his belly. "I haven't had a meal like that in a very long time," he said. "My compliments."

"I'll be sure to pass them along. Now, are you two going to be all archaic and take cigars and brandy in the study or something?" Sarcasm dripped from her lips, but she couldn't help it. Stephen's behavior was so cliché. Still, she knew it came from a place of love so she didn't protest too much. She'd need her family in the weeks and months ahead. Besides, maybe Jacob did need to have a conversation with one of her brothers. He was going to be connected to their family now forever.

Stephen rose and put his napkin on the table.

"No cigars for me, but I wouldn't say no to a drink. Jacob?"

"Ugh." Charlotte rolled her eyes. "Stephen, of all the times to play Lord of the Manor…"

He put a hand on her shoulder. "I am lord of this manor. And you are my sister. I'm just going to talk to him." He gave a squeeze. "Seriously, he used to be Special Forces. I'm not that dumb."

She couldn't help it, she snorted, and even Jacob grinned. "It's all right, Charlie. I'll find you later."

The two exited the dining room, leaving Charlotte sitting alone. She sighed. The last time Stephen had stepped into a relationship, it had nearly ruined everything. The situation with Jacob was tenuous enough without her brother's interference.

CHAPTER FOURTEEN

JACOB WATCHED STEPHEN CLOSELY, trying to get a read on his mood. He was definitely playing the protective brother, but Jacob didn't sense actual hostility or opposition. Stephen seemed relaxed as he went to a cabinet and took out a bottle.

"Brandy or whiskey?" Stephen asked.

"Whiskey," Jacob answered, and got a nod of approval.

Charlotte's brother gave Jacob a run for his money on physical build. The man was tall and in excellent shape, which Jacob found a bit surprising considering Stephen ran a fashion company with his mother and had a title after his name. But then, Jacob had learned long ago not to put too much stock in stereotypes.

While Charlie had lovely brown hair, Stephen's was almost black, and so were his eyes. It wouldn't take much more than a glare from him to intimidate people. Well, most people, anyway. Not Jacob.

He took the glass Stephen offered and lifted it in a casual toast before taking a sip.

It was excellent. But then, he expected no less from the Pembertons.

"So. You and my sister."

"I'm not sure how to answer that. Charlie and I haven't really discussed what our relationship is or will be. Yet."

Stephen gave a quick smile. "And I interrupted."

Jacob didn't answer, just lifted an eyebrow as they went to sit near the unlit fireplace. The whole room felt masculine to Jacob, and a way for Stephen to claim his dominance in the situation. Which made perfect sense to him. He was the outsider here; it was a position he was used to, so instead of making him uncomfortable, he felt in slightly familiar territory.

Stephen stared into his glass for several seconds before lifting his head and meeting Jacob's gaze. "I'm not sure how much you know about me or our family. Or if Charlotte told you about her twin, William, and what happened last fall."

"We haven't discussed it."

"I got in the way of my brother's happiness and acted in a way I'm not proud of. I don't want to repeat that mistake with Charlotte. At the same time, I'm her big brother, and I won't see her hurt."

"Having Charlie hurt is the last thing I want. She deserves to be happy."

"And you think that's with you?"

It was a fair question. Jacob took a gulp of whiskey and felt the burn straight to his gut. "Honestly, I don't know. She's a wonderful, rare woman, Stephen." He wasn't sure how much to reveal when he hadn't even revealed his feelings to Charlie herself. "The pregnancy was accidental. But as we move forward, nothing can be accidental. I want to do the right thing, for her and for our child."

"And is living in London while she's in Paris the right thing?"

The questions were getting tougher. "I ask myself that ten times a day."

Stephen fell silent, then sighed. "She loves you, you know."

A jolt of shock raced through Jacob's body and he sat forward. "She told you that?"

"She doesn't have to. We all saw the difference in her when she came back from New York. Not bad changes, just different. And her face when she talks about you or tonight when she looked at you."

This was news to him, and he wasn't sure what to do with it. "We've been talking about how to co-parent together. To do what's best for the baby. This weekend was supposed to be a time for us to really work that out."

Stephen nodded, unsmiling. "Bear in mind that Charlotte has never brought a man to either of our family homes, Jacob. This is a big deal for her."

"It's a big deal for me."

"Do you love her?"

He met Stephen's gaze. "I'm not sure it's your business if I do or not. I'm still...in shock." He sighed. "And surprised you haven't pointed out the fact that I'm not good enough for her."

Stephen chuckled then. "Well, of course you're not, I didn't think it bore mentioning." When Jacob bristled at the easy dismissal, Stephen waved a hand. "Listen, no one would be good enough for Charlotte. She's scary efficient but has a heart of gold. She'd do anything for her family and never wants to cause trouble. I see all of those things. For her to step out and make something her own, like she did with the crisis in New York, was unusual and very much needed, in my opinion. And I'm guessing you had something to do with that."

"Not really. I think it was in her all along. She just needed the crisis to make her rise to the occasion."

"And what about you? Is this going to make

you rise to the occasion, too? What are you willing to do to make Charlotte happy? To take
care of your family? Because that's what they
are now, even if you haven't put a ring on her
finger."

Jacob drained his glass. "You think I should
ask her to marry me."

"If you love her. And only if you love her.
Otherwise, set up some kind of parenting agreement. But don't give her false hope, Jacob. Her
heart's involved whether she wants it to be or
not."

Stephen got up to refresh their drinks, and
after he had done so, he reached into his pocket
and took out a small box. "I asked Maman and
she agreed. This is our grandmother's engagement ring. It is yours if you want to propose."

Jacob reached out and took the box, opening
the lid with a creak of the hinge. Inside was
nestled a gold band with a stunning square-cut
diamond in the middle, flanked by smaller diamonds in a fanciful pattern that looked like
delicate leaves. "It's beautiful."

Then he thought of the butterfly necklace
tucked into his duffel and his heart wrenched.
What was he going to do? Marriage was so
huge and would change his life irrevocably. But
then...so would parenthood. His stomach went

weightless as he realized after this weekend, nothing was going to be the same.

And he thought of Jacinta, and how he'd loved her, but how he didn't anymore.

"You look like someone knocked the wind out of you," Stephen observed, taking his seat again.

"Feels like it." He looked at Stephen, still reeling from the offer of the ring. "Stephen, I grew up in a regular old suburb, and I never had a whole lot growing up. I don't have a title, and even now I'm always on the outside of your world, even if I understand how it operates. That all being said, I hope you've offered this out of sentimentality and not because you think I can't afford to get Charlie the ring she deserves. Because I can."

"Hell, I know that. You don't think we researched Wolfe Security before we hired you? I don't give a damn if you were poor as a kid or if you know what fork to use. That's rubbish. What I care about is my sister. The ring is yours if you want it."

"I didn't expect the support."

"Mess this up and you'll see how quickly that goes away."

Jacob was starting to really like Stephen. They were a lot the same, despite the obvious differences. "Noted."

They sat in silence for a few minutes, sipping their drinks, until Jacob turned his head and looked at Stephen. He looked so Lord of the Manor, and yet what Jacob saw was a big brother looking out for his sister. Jacob liked to think he'd have done the same, if he'd had any siblings.

"She's lucky to have you, Stephen."

"Oh, I'm not so sure. I'm very, very flawed. But in this, I want to do right by her. She's taken our father's death hard, though she tries not to show it. It means something that she brought you here. Just talk to her." He turned languid eyes on Jacob. "And remember, I meant what I said. You hurt her, I'll mess you up. SAS or not."

"If I hurt her, I'll let you," Jacob said, and they went back to their drinks.

When Jacob suggested a walk in the garden after breakfast, Charlotte was more than happy to oblige. She'd missed seeing him last night after he'd disappeared with Stephen, and had lain awake wondering what they'd talked about, worried at Stephen's interference. But she hadn't risen from her bed to find out. The thought of disturbing Jacob in his room was far too tempting and she had to keep a clear head.

A walk in the garden was perfect.

A spring shower through the night left sparkling droplets on the leaves and flowers, and the fresh scent of moist earth and grass. As they walked along the path, Jacob reached out and took her hand. Clearly Stephen hadn't frightened Jacob away, and for that she was glad.

"The gardens here are so beautiful," he said. "I don't know the names of anything but the rosebushes, I don't think."

"The climbing vines with the light purple conical flowers? That's wisteria. And the big blooms on that frame there, the deep purple and white ones? Clematis." She pointed to her left. "And those showy pink blossoms are azaleas."

"You like the garden."

She nodded. "I do. When the verbena blooms, the butterflies go crazy for it. We have one section that is just florals that attract butterflies. Another that is all cutting flowers." She led him to the right, and pointed out another shrub, this one with flowers of the palest pink. "One of my favorites, camellias. Because the flowers are perfection."

"You're right. There's not one petal out of place."

She was quiet for a moment, searching for the right way to change the subject. "I see you made it through the conversation with Stephen last night."

"Your brother's a good man. And he cares about you very much. Actually, seeing you here explains a lot." They'd continued walking, but at a speed that could be considered only an amble. The morning sun felt glorious on her face. She had a baby growing inside her. Jacob was holding her hand. In a way, she wanted to hold on to this moment forever.

"Explains what?"

He shrugged. "You're yourself here. It suits you. For all your busy job and lifestyle, you like the simple things. Like sun and flowers and meat pies." He looked down at her and grinned. "Speaking of, breakfast settling okay?"

She nodded. "I do quite well with toast and tea."

When he pulled her off the path to stand beneath a whispery willow, she didn't resist. The grass was damp on her shoes, but she didn't care about that, either. Jacob looked like he had something to say. "What is it? We never finished talking last night. I was thinking, maybe the easiest thing would be to decide on terms and then have an agreement drawn up."

He reached for her other hand. "I think you should marry me."

Charlotte's whole body went numb. Marriage? When had that ever been on the table? She stared up at him, unable to speak, trying to sort out her thoughts. Elation at being asked, followed swiftly by dismay that he should propose because of the baby and not because of…love.

"I don't understand. What did Stephen say to you?"

His gray eyes were serious as they plumbed hers. "A lot of things. Mostly I think he was trying to get at how I feel about you. And the truth is, Charlie, I'm pretty sure I'm in love with you."

Just what she wanted, right? Then why was she more afraid than ever?

"In love with me? We spent a week together. And by your own admission, you're still in love with Jacinta." The way he winced as she said her name told her she was right. "Please, don't propose out of obligation or some warped version of doing the right thing."

He let go of her hands briefly. "Charlie, I've had to do a lot of thinking since I left you. And the truth is, I'm not in love with Jacinta. Not anymore. I did love her. Of course I did, or else it wouldn't have hurt so much when she died. But I've been hanging on to that guilt for years. It's kept me from moving forward. Until you. Until you, I was just kind of living a half life. Functioning but not really living at all."

She frowned, torn between wanting to believe him and knowing words were easy but actions harder. "I can't compete with a ghost, Jacob."

"You don't have to. Don't you see? It was my guilt holding me back, not love. I used it to keep people at arm's length. To not get involved. To not get hurt again. And then, at the airport in Paris… Well, walking away from you hurt. More than I ever expected."

And then he reached into his pocket and pulled out a familiar box.

Panic raced through her limbs. She hadn't expected this. Jacob wasn't the type to make flowery declarations and pull out diamonds. Stephen had to have persuaded him. She wanted him to love her but…oh, God. She wanted to believe in it. But she didn't. Because she knew without a doubt that if not for this baby, a proposal wouldn't even have crossed his mind.

He opened the box and she saw her grandmother's ring. Stephen had lied, then. He had known she was going to be here and came expressly for this purpose. She'd spent a lifetime doing the right thing for the family, and now that she'd finally broken free, the family wanted her to do the right thing for them again, didn't they? A neat-and-tidy marriage to the father of her baby.

"Charlie, will you marry me?"

She took a step back. "Don't be ridiculous. I—I can't. You shouldn't have asked. This isn't what we agreed."

His gray eyes widened, wounded. "Are you saying you don't love me? That what we shared wasn't real?"

The panic now felt like cold chills all over her body as she fought for breath. "So what if it was? It's a big leap from there to marriage. This makes no sense! We don't even live in the same country. And you... You willingly put yourself in danger! Are you willing to give all that up?"

"Are you asking me to?"

She didn't know how to answer. To her shock, she was afraid he'd say yes, he would give it up. Then what would he do? "I can't believe Stephen convinced you to do this," she breathed, shaking her head.

Jacob snapped the box closed and shoved it back in his pocket. "I know my own mind," he bit back. "Stephen may have given me the ring, but asking you was my choice. Because I thought we had something real. Because seeing you here, the way you kissed me yesterday, gave me hope. But I was wrong, wasn't I? Because even after everything that happened in New York, even after doing all that you asked this week when you told me about the baby, you don't trust me. And that's not something I can fix. That's something you have to do on your own. I'm not Mark, Charlie. I'm not after something, and I'm not your father. You're not going to lose me when you still need me. But you need to believe that, and you don't."

"You want me to trust you, when you're still hung up on Jacinta? You want me to believe you're ready for a relationship just like that? That you're ready for marriage? You say you won't leave me, but you're still determined to put yourself in danger in your job. Maybe this is just a chance for you to redeem yourself."

His voice softened, and sadness darkened his eyes. "Don't hide behind her because you're scared. I lost the one I loved, who loved me, because she was taken from me. But at least I didn't throw my chance away." He shook his head. "I understand if you don't love me. But I never imagined you'd be a coward."

"That's unfair." She lifted her chin. "You want to know why I don't trust you? Because when I returned to Paris, Maman told me you'd told her about the email. When you said you wouldn't."

"I never said I wouldn't. I said I wouldn't send it to your IT team and instead I'd send it to mine. I never agreed to not tell your mother. She was my employer. But you go ahead and tell yourself that's why because it'll make you feel better." His voice broke on the last word and he turned away.

"Jacob…"

He backed away, putting more distance between them. "I don't want to fight with you. Draft up a preliminary parental agreement and I'll have my lawyer look at it. I still plan to be a parent. I'm not abandoning you or my baby."

And then he turned and walked away, leaving her with a heart filled with confusion and a mountain of regret.

CHAPTER FIFTEEN

CHARLOTTE SAT IN numb silence. What on earth had happened this morning? One moment they were having a beautiful walk in the gardens and the next, everything had gone to pieces. She'd said things, horrible things, lashing out at him when he was right. She *was* scared. Terrified. Maybe if he'd eased his way into it, they'd talked, something… But she'd had no warning. No ability to prepare.

Now he was gone, without a word. Took his bag and got in his Land Rover and drove away, leaving her here with Stephen. They'd arrived together. For him to take off this way told her how very deeply she'd hurt him.

Perhaps that had been her first mistake. She hadn't realized she had the power to hurt him. He'd seemed so invincible, but he was not, was he?

There was a tap on her door, and then Stephen poked his head in. "May I come in?"

She nodded, wiping the tears away from below her eyes.

He sat on the bed next to her. "What the hell happened?"

"He proposed."

Stephen sat back a bit. "He did? Huh."

"I know you gave him the ring."

Stephen held out his hand and gave her the box. "Yes, with Maman's approval. What I don't understand is why you obviously said no and are now crying in your room about it."

"I don't understand, either!" She started to sob and he slid forward, putting his arm around her. "Why is it so hard to trust someone? To believe that he loves me?"

"Oh, sweetheart. Shall I give you a list?"

She chuckled through her tears, making a snorting sound. He straightened her up and looked directly into her face. "I am not the right one to answer that question. I'm hardly biased."

"I get it," she whispered. "I understand why you were so upset when your engagement with Bridget ended. I had something similar happen to me years ago, Stephen. Someone I thought I loved who was more interested in the Pemberton name than in me."

"I'm sorry. I know how much that hurts. Why did you never say?"

"I didn't want to upset the family. Cause

drama. Anyway, you had Gabi leave you, as well. So yeah, I get you not trusting."

He frowned then. "Look, with Gabi it was different. Part of why I was such a git was because it was a stupid plan in the first place. We were foolish to think we could marry to solve our problems. She's far more suited to William. But it does go to show something, Charlotte. That marrying for anything but love is a bad idea."

She sighed then, slightly comforted. "But how do you know? How do you trust that someone won't let you down?"

He rubbed her arm. "You don't. People are human and occasionally let each other down. But that brings me to the next entry on my list—Maman and Father."

Charlotte looked up, surprised. "What do you mean?"

"I know they had their share of arguments. They were two strong personalities with strong opinions. But have you ever seen anyone love harder or better? They set an almost impossible example to follow. And we Pembertons are a stubborn lot. If we can't do it the best, we don't want to do it at all. Because Pembertons don't fail."

"Except we do. All the time."

"Precisely. So really, the only question is, do you love him?"

Her insides trembled. "I do. It's the scariest feeling I've ever had in my life. I'm always the girl with a plan. Only now I don't have a plan. And I'm still scared, Stephen. I'm scared of what he does for a living. I'm scared to take that leap only to lose him. How do I survive that?"

"So you're willing to give up a chance at happiness just because sometime down the road he might possibly get hurt? Only you can decide if the risk is worth the reward. But I know you love him. And the way he spoke last night... He loves you, too. That doesn't mean there won't be obstacles. Maman is the better person to talk to about that. Do you think she would give up all her years with our dad if she'd known from the beginning that he'd die first?"

She shook her head. "Of course not."

"It just seems to me that you have a chance to have what you want and you're too afraid to reach out and take it when it's offered."

"He called me a coward."

"I'll beat him up for you."

That made her laugh.

Stephen patted her knee. "Come down for dinner. And then take some time to think. Honestly, I didn't think he'd propose today. I guess Jacob isn't the kind of guy to waste time."

No, because she knew to Jacob time was precious. Oh, there were so many feelings bubbling up within her that she didn't know what to think or do. But the idea of dinner appealed. She'd barely eaten, and she desperately needed something normal to help clear her mind a bit, sort out all the threads of her thoughts. "I'll meet you down there. Thank you, big brother. Wise counsel comes from the strangest places."

"Hey, easy when it's you. I'm not good at taking my own advice, though."

When he left, she got up and went to put the ring box on top of her dresser. It was then that she noticed the small Aurora bag. It hadn't been there before. She picked it up and inside was a white box tied with black ribbon.

And inside the box was a butterfly pendant on a chain, the bright gems sparkling in the spring sunlight filtering through her windows. A small note was tucked in beside it, and she put the necklace down gently and picked up the paper.

Picked this up in New York. It reminds me of you.
Don't let anyone clip your wings, Charlie.
Love, Jacob

He'd bought it in New York, back when they'd barely known each other. That day at the store? Perhaps… It was the only time they were apart during the trip. Even back then he'd had her on his mind, he'd seen into the deepest part of her and her longings. And now, when she'd hurled such horrible accusations at him, he still left her with words of love and encouragement.

He'd once said that he didn't deserve her. That he was wrong for her. But it was the other way around. She didn't deserve him.

Holding the butterfly in her hand, she wept into her pillow.

Jacob put his duffel down in his office and let out a big breath. This last trip had taken him to Egypt for a week, and he still felt dusty and hot. And tired. What he wanted was a shower and a steak, in that order.

And a drink. Maybe several. Being back on English soil only reminded him of Charlie, and he was still smarting from their last encounter. She'd disappointed him. Even though he understood every one of her fears, he'd hoped she'd rise above them and say yes. What a fool he was. What a stupid, romantic fool.

He chuckled mirthlessly as he sat in his desk chair and spun a little, surveying the otherwise empty office. No one in his life would ever accuse him of being romantic, but here he was, being what his men would call a "sad sack." Truth was, he was thirty-seven years old, and he'd given up the thought of a wife and family. Until Charlie came along. He could forget again, right? Build Wolfe Security up, maybe open a second and third office elsewhere. In the United States, maybe. Somewhere in the European Union.

The front door opened and he straightened, immediately alert. Was it Charlie, maybe? He rose, only to discover one of his logistical staff, MJ, was back to grab something they'd forgotten for the weekend.

"Sorry, boss," they said, retrieving their backpack. "Can't believe I left this here. Good trip?"

"Good trip," he replied, attempting a smile. "Hot."

"Not great for having a delayed flight, either, huh? We expected you a few hours ago. So did someone else, who came looking for you."

"Who?" He sat up straighter.

"A woman, dark hair, pretty. About my age."

Since MJ was still in their twenties, he couldn't stop his heart from wondering if it was Charlie. "Did she leave a name?"

MJ shook their head. "But she did say she'd come back later, that she'd probably head to the pub to wait. She didn't say which pub, though."

He knew which one. "Thanks, MJ."

"Have a good weekend, boss."

When they were gone, he got up from his

chair and paced. What was she doing here? Dare he hope? Or perhaps she was just delivering the agreement he'd suggested she have drafted. He closed his eyes. He had to deal with her sometime. The job in Mansoura had been a distraction, but now that he was back, Charlie and their child was all he could think about.

He grabbed his bag and headed upstairs for a quick shower. He didn't even wait for the shower to run—hot water was overrated—and in five minutes he was dressed and downstairs again, trying to sort out in his brain what he was going to say.

And when he opened the door, he jumped back when he saw her standing there, her hand raised to knock, a startled look on her face.

"You were at the pub," he said, then wondered if he could sound more like an idiot.

"I was. And then I thought I'd try again. One of your staff said your flight had been delayed."

"A couple of hours, yeah."

She nodded. And then he clued in and stepped back. "You'd better come in."

She stepped over the threshold carefully, looking around. "This really is a lovely space," she said quietly. "The last time I was here it was dark and I didn't really look around."

"Thanks." He wanted to ask why she was there, but figured she'd get to it eventually.

She bit down on her lip. "I, uh, can we talk?" Her hazel eyes slipped up to meet his. "The last time… We didn't leave things very well."

It hurt to see her, right in the middle of his chest, but he had to figure out a way to deal with it, for their child's sake. "Of course we can. Do you want to go upstairs or go for a walk?"

She smiled up at him. "Would it be odd to say I'd like to sit on one of those benches on the Green?"

"It's a beautiful afternoon. Of course not."

He locked the door behind him and they crossed the street, walking along the perimeter of the Green until they found an empty bench. A group of teenagers were having a game of football and their shouts punctuated the air, a pleasant sound that reminded Jacob of childhood summers and a time when life was, if not carefree, at least less complicated.

"Jacob, I'm sorry." She reached over and took his hand. "I'm sorry for all the things I said that morning in the garden. I'm sorry I hurt you. I'm sorry for so much."

His throat tightened. "I…don't know what to say."

"Say you'll forgive me."

"I forgave you a long time ago. I forgave you before I ever left."

"When you wrote the note that came with

this?" She moved the collar of her blouse to reveal the butterfly necklace, which winked in the sunlight.

It looked perfect on her, just as he'd imagined. "Yes," he murmured. "When I wrote that note."

"But you still left."

He lifted his gaze from the necklace to her eyes. "I was hurting, Charlie."

To his surprise, her eyes filled with tears. "I know. I'm sorry. You asked and I panicked and I said everything wrong."

"I'm not sure there's a right way to say it," he said, and looked away.

"There were things I should have said, too," she whispered, reaching for his hand. "Like I love you. Like I'm scared to death. Oh, Jacob, I wasn't ready for that."

"Then tell me what you need. I've gone over and over it in my head and the only way we're going to be able to move forward is if we're completely honest with each other."

She nodded, blinked away the tears. "You're right. And you were right that day, too. I threw a lot of stuff at you out of fear, but the truth is I was too afraid to trust in it. That part is on me. What I need from a partner is just…honesty. To know that I—and my child—come first. I know you don't have an agenda where I'm concerned. In fact, I'm pretty sure the fact that I'm a Pemberton and Aurora Germain's daughter is a complication and not a perk."

He smiled then. Honesty and putting her first? Easy.

Charlotte wasn't sure why Jacob was suddenly smiling. This was by far the hardest thing she'd ever done, especially considering she was still afraid. Over the past weeks she'd come to realize that guarantees were impossible. That loving Jacob wasn't something that was going away. They were having a child together. She had no idea what a relationship with him would look like…what marriage would look like, but she had to try.

"Charlie," he said, his voice warm and sure, "you and our child will always come first. I meant what I said about the past. It's been far more about guilt than love for a long time. It took you coming along to make me see it. I know this has happened fast, but sometimes you just know. That night, with you, it all just clicked. I walked away because I thought it was what you wanted. But in Paris, I nearly missed my flight to London because I wanted to go after you."

Her heart leaped. "I wish you had."

"Me, too, now. But in a way you were right. I wasn't ready. It wasn't until I was without you that I realized how deep my feelings ran. In

New York you said I was worthy of redemption, but I'd never felt so until that moment. You changed me. How could I not love you?"

"Then why didn't you fight harder?" Tears did come now, quiet ones, and she dipped her head because they were in public. Maybe this would have been better inside. She'd thought being in the park would preclude this kind of emotion.

"Because I knew it was pointless if you couldn't trust me. I was hurting, too. I felt like I'd laid my heart at your feet and you kicked it back at me."

Shame slid into her heart, along with regret, knowing she'd caused him such pain. "You don't have to defend yourself against what I said that day," she whispered. "I never should have said it. Especially about you telling Maman about the email. I used it against you, but Jacob, you telling her demonstrates how much integrity you've got. I admire it, even if I was angry about it."

"You were scared. You are scared. You don't like what I do. I get that, because I went through a lot of sleepless nights as a kid when my dad was on duty."

"It's part of who you are. I get that." The anxiety was real, but he'd helped her step into her own. How could she demand that he be less than he was?

"Maybe, but it's not all I am. Charlie, any relationship takes compromise. I know that. So here's what I'm thinking... I stop taking field assignments. If it makes you more secure, I can do that, no problem."

She hadn't expected that. She'd expected another version of "I could get hit by a bus" but instead he was ready to make a sacrifice. Was she?

She looked around at the wide green space, thought about how close they were to Chatsworth Manor, and knew she could also easily adjust her life. "You'd do that for me? For us?"

"In a heartbeat," he said.

Hope started to spiral in her heart. She squeezed his hands and looked into his oh-so-handsome face. "I can base out of London. We could..." She swallowed and hoped that she wasn't presuming too much. "We could live here. I can keep the flat in Paris for when I need to be there, and we'll be close to the estate, too. I can do my job from here and videoconference when I need to."

"You'd leave Paris?"

"Compromise," she said, and a smile started to bloom on her lips. Was this really going to work?

He slid over closer to her and hesitantly rested his hand on her still-flat tummy. "I hadn't considered fatherhood before. Now I can't think of anything else. I want to be with this little one, watch them grow. Can we do that together, do you think?"

The hope that had been growing in her heart expanded into happiness. "I know we can." She reached into her small purse and took out an envelope. "Look. I got you a printed copy." He opened the envelope and took out the image of the twelve-week scan she'd just had done.

"This is our baby?"

She nodded, tears threatening again. "I didn't ask to know the gender. I didn't know if you'd want to. I kind of hoped that it was something we could find out together."

"I can't...this is...wow." He sat back on the bench, his face full of wonder and awe. "You and I did this."

She nodded.

"If we did this, we can do anything."

She was feeling that, too. So she reached down into her bag and took out one more thing.

"Jacob? I know it's a little unorthodox, but... Will you marry me?" She held out the little box that contained the ring he'd proposed with only weeks earlier.

He took the tiny box from her fingers and opened it. Nerves—the good kind—swirled around in her stomach. She'd been so afraid that she'd ruined everything that day in the Chatsworth gardens, but Jacob's love for her had been bigger than her fear. Maybe that was all she really had to know.

He picked the ring out from the slot and held it in his fingers, then reached for her hand. "Yes, I'll marry you. The sooner the better. I don't intend to let you get away again."

He slid the ring over her knuckle and she stared at it there, then blinked away tears. Her father would have loved Jacob. And her grandparents would have been so pleased. Their own love story had been one for the books—a whirlwind romance during the 1958 flu pandemic, when he'd been ill and she'd been a nurse. They'd married one week after his recovery.

She'd tell Jacob that story one day, but not today. Today was for them.

"I love you," she whispered, rubbing her thumb over the bright diamonds.

"And I love you." He leaned forward and kissed her, in the way she liked best: slow, soft, tender. And then he leaned back and opened his arm, welcoming her into his embrace as they breathed in the early summer air and watched the football game, with everything right in their world.

CHAPTER SIXTEEN

THE CHATSWORTH GARDENS were glorious on the first Saturday in June. The immediate Pemberton family was seated in white chairs, waiting for the bride, while butterflies and bees flitted around them, sipping on the showy blossoms.

Charlotte stood just inside the garden doors, her hand firm on Stephen's sleeve. Stephen, who had nearly cried when she'd asked him to give her away. Bella and Jacob's father, Ian, were serving as witnesses. The wedding was small, intimate and certainly not what was expected for a Pemberton. But it was exactly what she wanted. The people she loved most in the place she loved most.

"Are you ready?" Stephen asked. "I just got the signal from the officiant."

She nodded. She was so ready. It had been only two weeks from proposal to ceremony and even then it had seemed too long. Her dress was deceptively simple, a sleeveless white A-line with a tiny train and detail just on the shoulders. It was an Aurora design, of course, and her favorite from last year's bridal collection straight off the rack. Her bouquet was cut from the garden, the last of the lilacs and best of the roses. A simple camellia was in her hair. There'd be a celebration following the service, and then she and Jacob would be heading to Tenerife for their honeymoon. That had been her idea, since she'd caused him to miss his first trip.

"Thank you, Stephen. For this. For interfering." She smiled up at him. "You got it right this time."

"As long as you're happy, I'm happy."

She didn't quite believe him. Stephen was lonely, and they all knew it. But he'd have to solve that in his own time.

"Shall we?"

The doors were opened and Stephen and Charlotte stepped outside into the bright sunlight. Jacob was waiting at the rose trellis, his gray eyes shining and a smile lighting up his face as she appeared. When they reached him and Stephen gave Jacob her hand, she realized hers was trembling. His was not. He was, and always would be, her rock.

She wanted to kiss him so much right now, but first there were vows to be said.

"I, Jacob Andrew Wolfe, take you, Charlotte Louise Pemberton…"

She would not cry. She wouldn't.

"…to have and to hold, from this day forward…"

Someone sniffled. Charlotte looked into Jacob's eyes and heard the words, but more, she felt them, deep inside, where she would cherish them always.

"I, Charlotte Louise Pemberton, take you, Jacob Andrew Wolfe…"

Her voice shook as she repeated the words. After this moment, he would be hers, and she would be his. Forever. She wasn't sure how she'd gotten so lucky, but she promised herself to be thankful every day.

"…till death us do part."

They exchanged rings…and then the moment she'd been waiting for…the kiss to seal the deal. And just when she was sure her heart couldn't get any fuller, he placed his palm on her stomach before leaning in to touch her lips with his. "I love you," he whispered. "Both of you."

"We love you, too," she replied, and tilted her face up for her first kiss as his wife.

* * * * *

If you missed the previous story in the
Heirs to an Empire trilogy,
then check out

Scandal and the Runaway Bride

And if you enjoyed this story,
check out these other great reads from
Donna Alward

The Billionaire's Island Bride
Beauty and the Brooding Billionaire
Christmas Baby for the Billionaire

All available now!